It's a battle be

The life of the king of the island kingdom of Zaki hangs in the balance after a major cardiac event leaves him needing life-saving surgery.

Neither of his two sons, princes Raed and Amir, are ready to return home to step into their father's shoes. Raed because he has the career he has always dreamed of as a neurosurgeon in London, and Amir because he and daughter, Farah, are still recovering from the terrible accident that claimed the life of his wife.

But when duty calls, the sons must answer.

And love? Well, love always finds a way…

Fall in love with Raed and Soraya in
Surgeon Prince's Fake Fiancée

Discover what awaits Amir and Isolde in
A Mother for His Little Princess

Both available now!

Dear Reader,

As a member of the royal family in the island kingdom of Zaki, Prince Raed should have been living in luxury. But life in the palace isn't as idyllic as it is in fairy tales and he's given it up to work in a London hospital.

When his father's ill health threatens to derail the monarchy, he persuades colleague Soraya to pose as his fake fiancée to provide a distraction in the press. Both reeling from recent breakups, a relationship for either of them is the last thing they want, but they have no choice when there's so much at stake.

As the eldest in their families, they have shouldered responsibility their entire lives, putting other people's happiness before their own. Together they find the emotional support and understanding in one another that's been missing for so long.

But with a clash of cultures and the couple torn between London life and exotic Zaki, making it work seems impossible. Love can't solve everything, can it?

I hope you enjoy Raed and Soraya's journey to find love and their true calling.

Happy reading!

Karin x

SURGEON PRINCE'S FAKE FIANCÉE

KARIN BAINE

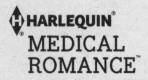

HARLEQUIN®
MEDICAL
ROMANCE™

Recycling programs
for this product may
not exist in your area.

ISBN-13: 978-1-335-59518-8

Surgeon Prince's Fake Fiancée

Copyright © 2023 by Karin Baine

For questions and comments about the quality of this book, please contact us at CustomerService@Harlequin.com.

Harlequin Enterprises ULC
22 Adelaide St. West, 41st Floor
Toronto, Ontario M5H 4E3, Canada
www.Harlequin.com

Printed in U.S.A.

Karin Baine lives in Northern Ireland with her husband, two sons and her out-of-control notebook collection. Her mother and her grandmother's vast collection of books inspired her love of reading and her dream of becoming a Harlequin author. Now she can tell people she has a *proper* job! You can follow Karin on Twitter @karinbaine1 or visit her website for the latest news, karinbaine.com.

Books by Karin Baine

Harlequin Medical Romance

Carey Cove Midwives

Festive Fling to Forever

One Night with Her Italian Doc
The Surgeon and the Princess
The Nurse's Christmas Hero
Wed for Their One Night Baby
A GP to Steal His Heart
Single Dad for the Heart Doctor
Falling Again for the Surgeon
Nurse's Risk with the Rebel

Harlequin Romance

Pregnant Princess at the Altar

Visit the Author Profile page
at Harlequin.com for more titles.

For my prince xx

CHAPTER ONE

'WHAT THE…? WHAT, NOW?'

Soraya's head was spinning, partly from the information that had just been launched at her, but mostly from being ushered into a small office at top speed by someone who usually didn't have two words to say to her. At least not pleasant ones.

'I need you to operate on my father.'

Raed Ayad, a neurosurgeon who worked at the hospital, and someone she'd had the misfortune to run into on occasion, sighed as he repeated his demand.

He was slightly less frantic now than when he'd first accosted her in the corridor, asked her for 'a quick word', then corralled her into this room. After the rambling about a country in need and his responsibility, at least now he was clarifying what he wanted from her. She just didn't know why.

It was an open secret that Raed, super surgeon, was also a prince in his own country. An island in the Persian Gulf somewhere that apparently wasn't missing him. Although his royal status was something she could have guessed by the regal way he glided through the hospital corridors. Goodness knew why he was working in a busy London hospital if he had a luxurious palace somewhere to lounge around in. Some people didn't have a choice but to work day and night to pay the bills, but at least she only had herself to support now the divorce had come through. Still, she had a lot on her mind, what with the debt her cheating ex-husband had run up, moving into her sister's tiny flat, and transferring to the London Central Hospital. Getting involved in Raed's family drama wasn't something she needed on top of that.

Especially when he'd been so rude to her when she'd asked him for his help not so long ago. She'd been trying to raise funds for a young local carers' charity to provide a centre where they could go for respite. Something that was close to her heart as she'd cared for her elderly, ailing parents and taken on the responsibility of her younger sister, Isolde, in her teens. New to the hospital, and the area, she'd targeted her fellow surgeons during her fundraising, knowing they had a bigger income than most of the medical staff. When she had approached Raed during the fundraising day, dressed in her pyjamas, her hair tied in pigtails and her front tooth blacked out, he'd snapped, 'Not now,' and stomped off down the corridor. For a prince, he'd been sadly lacking in manners.

'Tell me again what's going on. Slowly.'

His breath of frustration and clenched jaw did little to win Soraya's sympathy.

'My father's in the hospital. He's had a heart attack and needs a bypass operation.'

'Okay, but what does that have to do with me?' Apart from his complete dismissal of her charity fundraising, she was pretty sure this was the first time he'd actually spoken to her directly. Usually he swept into the hospital, worked his magic in the operating theatre, then swept out again, leaving everyone in awe behind him. His reputation was second to none, at least professionally speaking. He wasn't known for being personable. Cool, precise and controlled were usually the words used to describe him. The nicer ones at least.

Raed was tugging at his hair now, mussing the usually sleek raven locks. Even the carefully groomed beard he sported seemed a little unruly today. 'My father is the King. If anything happens to him, our country will be in uproar. We need to keep this quiet until we know he's going to be all right. You're the best cardiac surgeon the trust has.'

She couldn't argue with that, yet she held a little resentment that he'd clearly had privileges to get where he was in his career, when she'd had to struggle every day. A prince wouldn't have had to work menial jobs to pay for schooling, or raise a sister alone after their parents died, or sell a home to pay off a cheating ex's debts.

Okay, so none of that was Raed's fault, but if he weren't so arrogant she wouldn't have taken such a dislike to him. Not that she would let her personal feelings get in the way of her doing her job.

'I'll check my schedule.'

'You don't understand, there is no time.' He was pacing the room now, which brought back memories for her. She'd been equally worried when both of her parents had been ill. Although a patient still had a chance if they received a heart bypass. Terminal lung cancer was somewhat more difficult to reconcile. Especially when both of her parents had succumbed to it within a year of each other.

'I know you're upset, Raed. Why don't you sit down and we can talk about this?' She tried to direct him towards a seat but he simply resumed pacing.

'Don't you see? I'm the next in line to the throne. If he dies I have to go back.'

This was the first time she'd seen Raed anything other than cool and in control and it was clear he was in a crisis. Not least because he'd chosen her to confide in.

'Surely, that's not news to you? I mean, I don't know much about your country but if you're next in line to the throne...'

'It was supposed to be Amir but I can't expect him to go back now.'

'Ah, yes, your brother? I was sorry to hear about the accident and the loss of your sister-in-law. My sister, Isolde, is working with your niece on her mobility issues.' Soraya remembered the story about the car crash being on the news, back before Raed had been in her orbit. Isolde had recently been working with Farah, his nine-year-old niece, who was still struggling to walk six months on. It was clear the family had been through a lot recently.

'So you know he can't go back. He's not in the right head space to run a country and he's needed here. I—I just need some more time.' He finally dropped into the chair, seemingly defeated by his circumstances, and Soraya couldn't help but feel sorry for him.

'Forgive me, but aren't you the eldest? *Shouldn't* it be you?' Surely he'd had a lifetime to prepare for this role? Soraya didn't understand why it seemed to come as such a surprise now.

'Amir was going to take my position as rightful heir. We were about to make an official announcement to surrender my right to be next in line to the throne when the accident happened. Of course we've had to delay that because he has to focus on Farah, but, with my father ill now, someone will have to go back to Zaki. I guess that's going to be me.' The reluctance was there in every word, but also an acceptance that this was his fate as the eldest son.

Although she wasn't royalty, Soraya knew how it was to be so burdened by responsibility, given she'd spent most of her life looking after her younger sister. Their parents had had them late in life, their health gradually declining when Soraya was a teenager, so she'd parented Isolde even before they'd been orphaned, putting her sister's needs before her own. It was clear Raed had a life here in London, including a successful career, that he didn't want to leave behind, but it appeared he had no choice. That familiar pressure awakened a new empathy towards him.

'Okay, okay. I'll go and see your father and talk to his consultant.'

'Thank you, Soraya.'

She didn't know if it was the unfamiliar sound of her name on his tongue or the look of gratitude in those deep brown eyes that made her legs wobble beneath her jade-green wrap dress as she left the room. Not a development she was excited about when she was still getting over her marriage break-up.

It had been only fourteen months since her whole world had come crashing down, when she found out, not only that Frank had cheated on her, but also that he'd funded it with her money. Romance had been the last thing on her mind when she'd been busy with work and raising Isolde, and though there'd been a few dates and disasters in medical school her priorities had lain elsewhere, so it wasn't until Isolde had grown up and moved out that she'd been open to the idea of sharing her life with someone else. Frank had been her first real relationship.

He was a lawyer who specialised in helping charitable causes, and she'd thought him a man she could trust, who would put her before anything else as he clearly had such a big heart. Wrong.

She'd thought, because he was so generously

giving his time and effort to good causes, it was only right that they would live off her earnings. What she'd been unaware of was the fact that he was giving a lot more to one of his administrators than paperwork, and running up credit in both their names to fund his affair.

Isolde had wanted her to go to the police and have him charged with fraud for forging her signature on loans and credit agreements, which she'd later found out paid for luxury holidays and expensive hotels. When she'd believed he was away fighting for funding and debating issues with parliament, he'd actually been living it up with his mistress. Despite all that she didn't want a long, drawn-out court case where she'd have to face Frank and his lies all over again. It was more important to her to cut her losses and walk away. Even if that meant selling her home to do so and taking up residence in her little sister's box room in the meantime.

All that trauma and upset meant she wasn't in any hurry to even think about another man. If and when she was ready to get close to someone else, it would be with a man who would put her first for a change. Certainly not one who had the weight of an entire country on his shoulders.

Royalty was a world away from the life she

led, but when she operated on his father she would treat him as every other patient. And Raed? He was just another attractive, successful, concerned family member she would probably never have to deal with again.

Raed stayed in the chair long after the blaze of Soraya's red hair had disappeared out of sight. There was a definite sense of relief easing the tension from his body now that she'd agreed to perform his father's surgery, but it was mixed with the shame of his emotional outburst. In their line of work it was nothing new to have relatives breaking down on them, but Soraya was a colleague, one he didn't know particularly well. That hadn't stopped him blabbing some very personal details he'd clearly been bottling up for too long though.

It had been a long couple of days, watching his father fighting for his life, and inwardly dealing with all the consequences of that. At least he'd been stabilised now, even if he needed that all-important heart bypass. In the meantime, it was down to Raed how they publicly dealt with the situation.

He'd been under pressure to return to the family fold ever since the car crash that had devastated his brother Amir's life. Responsibility to his family and his country had already cost him his relationship, but he wasn't ready to leave his whole life behind here in England just yet. And he knew if they revealed his father's serious health woes his countrymen would expect him to immediately go home and take up the reins, which would be no mean feat. It was something Amir had been preparing for, not Raed.

He took his phone out of his pocket and called his brother.

'How did it go?' Amir knew his plan to get Soraya onside to give their father the best chance of surviving.

'She's on board, though it took a little grovelling.'

His brother gave a brittle laugh. Raed didn't think he'd heard him truly laugh since his wife had died. 'Now *that* I would like to have seen.'

'It wasn't my finest moment.' He cringed, thinking about the display he'd put on. Usually he was able to keep a lid on his feelings. Even when Zara had left him, unable to deal with the idea of potentially having to move back home with him and become part of the royal family, he hadn't made a scene like that. His emotions were usually the one thing in his life he could keep control over.

From a very young age his whole life had been dictated by his royal role—until he'd rebelled against his position and decided to go into medicine, making his own path. He'd worked hard to be a success, but this just proved he still had no control of his own life. And now he'd loosened his grip on those emotions he usually tried so hard to keep to himself in front of a colleague, it felt as though everything was slipping away from him again.

He supposed it was the culmination of everything hitting him all at once, plus lack of sleep. Add to that the initial hostility towards him from the one person who might have been able to help them get through this nightmare, and he'd lost his usual composure. In that moment when it had seemed as though she wasn't going to make things easy for him, he'd seen himself on the first private jet home. Alone. Leaving his family and all their problems here without him. Despite Soraya's help there was no knowing if his father would survive, his mother was in bits, and Amir and Farah needed his support. Even if he could walk away from his career and the independent life he'd made for himself here, he was torn between the responsibility he felt towards his family, and that for his country. His life was never going to be his own again.

'Well, we're all struggling, Raed.'

'How is Mother? Sorry I had to leave but I wanted to catch Dr Yarrow.'

'I know, don't worry. I've sent her back to the hotel to rest.'

'Good idea. A five-star suite with an entourage to take care of her is a lot better than sitting in a tiny family room with a cup of cold coffee waiting for news. Something Mother is not used to, even if the two of us spend a lot of time in those situations. Albeit on the other end of the conversations that tend to happen in the family room.' His brother was a thoracic surgeon who often worked in life-or-death situations too. Both he and Amir had gone to England for medical school and were working in the same hospital. For now. Neither of them knew what the future held.

'We all need some rest or we won't be any use to Father at all. Listen, I'll be in with Farah for her physiotherapy appointment tomorrow. Why don't you get some sleep tonight and come and say hello tomorrow?'

'I might just do that,' Raed said and ended the call.

Before that he'd check in with his mother to make sure she was all right, and get an update on his father from his consultant. He needed to be with his family. After all, he didn't know how much longer he'd have left with them.

* * *

'Hey, Fa-Fa.' Raed greeted his young niece with the nickname he knew she secretly loved even when she pulled that face at him. He hadn't slept any better last night than he had by his father's bedside when he'd been first admitted to the cardiac unit, but he put on a brave face for Farah so she didn't unduly worry. He supposed his brother and mother were also trying to shield her from the possibility of losing another loved one. She knew her grandfather was ill, but they hadn't shared any critical details in the hope he would recover before she realised how sick he really was.

'Hi, Uncle Raed.' Farah smiled, though these days there was a sadness in it that broke his heart.

He kissed her on the cheek. 'So, how's it going?'

She screwed up her nose. 'It's not fun.'

'I know, sweetheart, but these exercises are all to try and make your legs stronger.'

'What's the point if I'm never going to walk again?' It was tough to see her so despondent in the wheelchair, as though she'd given up. She wasn't the same energetic child who used to dance on his feet while holding his hands, giggling and singing. Even though there was a chance she could regain full use of her limbs, he wasn't so sure he'd get that fun-loving niece back again. That crash had stolen so much from her—and Amir—and Raed wished he could do something to make them happy again. Something he wouldn't be able to do if he was on the other side of the world from them.

'We're working on it, Farah, aren't we?' a perky young blonde said as she came into the room. She clearly knew his niece and, judging by the uniform, he assumed it must be the physiotherapist helping her with her rehabilitation.

'Raed, this is Isolde.' It was Amir who introduced her and Raed didn't miss the smile on his face as he did so.

'Isolde? That's not a name I've heard before, yet I think that's the second time in a couple of days... Is Dr Yarrow your sister?' It slowly dawned on him as he saw the family resemblance that Soraya had mentioned something about her sister working with Farah.

'Yes. I'm supposed to be meeting her for lunch once I'm finished up here. Speak of the devil...' Isolde turned her head and Raed followed her gaze to see Soraya waving from the door.

'We'll let you go. I'm sure you have a lot to catch up on.' The sight of her immediately made him cringe at the thought of their conversation yesterday. She'd witnessed him at his worst, his most vulnerable, a side of him neither his patients nor his family had ever seen. It had been a moment of weakness he hoped never to repeat, or be reminded of again.

'Can Isolde come to lunch with us, Papa?' Farah, who'd been quiet during the exchange around her, now spoke up to torpedo Raed's plan to try and avoid the Yarrow sisters as much as possible.

'Ms Yarrow just said she already has plans with her sister,' Amir countered, clearly as uncomfortable with the idea as he was.

'Soraya moved into my tiny flat with me last year so we're sick of the sight of each other. Only joking. It would be nice to have some company other than my bossy big sister and it makes sense for us all to have lunch together.' Isolde looked as thrilled with the idea as his niece, and Raed knew they were fighting a losing battle.

Both he and Amir would do anything to make Farah smile again. Even if it meant asking Soraya to join them too. Sitting through a lunch with a colleague he'd embarrassed himself in front of seemed a small price to pay for his niece's happiness.

'We're having afternoon tea at Grandmother's hotel with scones and tiny sandwiches and macarons.'

'Sounds lovely.' Isolde was grinning at Farah's unexpected excitement over such a simple thing as lunch.

It was clear to see the pair had quickly built up a rapport and, though his brother probably wasn't ready to socialise just yet, Raed thought it would be worth both their personal discomfort to keep that smile on Farah's little face a while longer.

'Of course you and your sister should join us for lunch. As a thank you for helping us, and we are all work colleagues after all.' He took the initiative, realising he would have to face Soraya again sooner or later as they'd probably be seeing more of each other because of his father.

Isolde rushed over to offer the lunch invitation to her sister and he watched the puzzled look on her face turn into one of irritation. Then she saw he was watching and forced a smile as she waved over.

With a little prompting from Isolde, Soraya came into the room to join them. 'Thank you so much for the invite but—'

'But nothing,' Isolde interrupted her sister. 'We are going for afternoon tea with the lovely royal family, Soraya.'

The pointed look Isolde gave her almost made Raed laugh out loud and he had to turn away so they wouldn't see the smirk on his face. It was clear who really called the shots in this sibling relationship and it made him feel better to see her on the back foot this time.

'We would have to go and get changed first, Isolde, and I don't really have time to take out of my day,' Soraya insisted through gritted teeth.

'You look absolutely fine, and it'll be a private affair. We won't be expected to dine with the public, don't worry. There is a car waiting to take us there and it can bring you straight back after lunch so you don't miss any work. You are allowed a lunch break, Soraya.' Despite previously embarrassing himself, and not wishing to revisit it in her presence, there was a greater part of Raed that was enjoying seeing her discomfort. It proved the great Dr Yarrow was human too.

Soraya Yarrow had an excellent reputation for her surgery skills and for working well in a crisis. Which was partly why he was cringing at the memory of his mini emotional breakdown when it had looked as though he couldn't hold it together.

'Thank you. That's very kind.' She smiled graciously but there was a tension in her body that couldn't disguise her annoyance.

It was obvious she didn't want to have lunch

with him and Amir, but here she was, trapped by her loyalty to her sibling. He knew something about that. Hopefully her unease would go some way to cancelling his out, then they might even be able to enjoy their meal. Although he did enjoy seeing her lose her cool, proving he wasn't the only one who could have an off day.

Dr Yarrow had a good reputation in the hospital. He'd asked around, and apparently she had joined the staff around the same time he'd split with Zara. He didn't recall meeting her before, but he hadn't been in the mood for much conversation with anyone at that time. His mind had been full of worries about his future, where he was going to end up, and how he was going to get through it all without any support. As usual he'd simply had to push his emotions to one side and get on with things. The same thing he'd been doing from a young age when it came to public appearances, or when he was sent to boarding school away from his family. He hadn't been allowed to say he was unhappy, and had been expected to carry on regardless.

So when Zara had called it quits on their relationship and moved out, he'd gone back to work and helped those who still needed him. It hadn't meant he wasn't hurting on the inside. Just like now.

He would try and make friends, share a meal with the woman who would hopefully save his father's life, but he was still frightened half to death about what was coming next for him too.

CHAPTER TWO

'THE ONLY THING more intimidating than having to perform heart surgery on a king is probably having afternoon tea with the rest of his family,' Soraya grumbled to her sister.

'It'll be fine. Amir and Farah are sweethearts,' Isolde replied, trying to reassure her this wasn't going to be the awkward, forced meal she was expecting.

'It's not Amir or Farah I'm worried about. Raed has that air of superiority about him at the hospital at the best of times, but this is about his royal status today. We're going to be in the presence of his mother, the Queen. I'm sure he'll use the opportunity to lord it over us peasants.'

Soraya was sure he'd want to claw back some dignity after his emotional outburst yesterday. Men like him usually did that by lashing out at those lesser mortals around them. Since she'd been the one to witness his moment of vulnerability, it stood to reason she'd be the one in the firing line. Not that she could explain that to Isolde when Raed had come to her in confidence.

'You worry too much. Just enjoy the ride, sis,' Isolde told her as they followed the Ayad family out of the hospital and into the back of the luxury car sent to pick them up.

Raed, back to his usual self, barely acknowledged her presence. That was why his emotional plea for her to help his family had been unexpected, as was discovering he did indeed hold her work in high regard. Though she would never have guessed he even knew her name until today. It was clear events with his father had shaken him, unravelling that usual cool façade.

She understood that; she'd been through the deaths of both of her parents, and that feeling of helplessness had helped spur her on to work in the medical profession. The frustration of his father's fate being completely out of his control was understandable. Especially when it was obviously going to impact on his life too. Though she sympathised, there was little she could do to help, other than perform the surgery and hope everything turned out the way he wanted.

She supposed he hadn't intended to share such deeply personal information with her during their short meeting yesterday, but it was also something he'd apparently needed to get off his chest. When she'd turned up to meet Isolde for lunch, she'd seen the way he'd flinched at the sight of her again. Something she was trying not to take personally, aware that he was probably embarrassed by what he had shared with her, and appearing vulnerable to a colleague he barely knew.

So it was baffling why he'd pushed her into coming for this meal. Unless he just wanted to see her squirm too.

'It looks as though it might rain this afternoon,' Raed finally said, breaking the silence in the car.

'Yes. Thank goodness we didn't decide on an al fresco lunch.' Soraya gave a fake laugh at her own lame joke.

'It could have ended up a complete washout,' Amir offered into the small talk.

The short car journey to the hotel should have been something to crow about for the rest of her days, speeding through the streets of London like VIPs in a swanky limo. Yet even with the five of them spread out across the luxurious black leather interior, conversation was stilted, the atmosphere awkwardly tense, because most of those in the car had no desire to be there. With the exception of Farah and Isolde, who were chatting like old friends, oblivious to everyone else now staring out of the windows and avoiding eye contact with nothing left to say to one another.

It was typical of Isolde to drag her along to something she had no interest in, yet she didn't have the heart to refuse her sister. Isolde was something of a free spirit and prone to acting impulsively, causing no end of worry to Soraya. Probably because Isolde had grown up without the burden of household bills, schooling, and learning to parent when she was barely an adult herself. Whereas Soraya had had all that worry and anxiety that came with raising a child without ever having had a choice in the matter.

She wasn't jealous of the freedom her younger sister had without that burden of guilt and responsibility. If anything she was glad it hadn't continued down the family line and ended with her. Isolde got to live the life they both should have been afforded, though ultimately Soraya had been forced to sacrifice her freedom for her sibling to have it. From time to time she did wonder what it would feel like to live without a care in the world. Like now, afternoon tea was such a small thing, albeit with some influential people. And, while Isolde was relishing every moment, Soraya was the one worrying about the impression they would

make. If they would measure up. Or if Raed
and his family would see them for the commoners they were.

'Isn't this amazing?' Isolde exclaimed as they
walked into the hotel, clearly dazzled by the
opulence around them.

'It's a sickening display of wealth and privilege.' It wasn't as easy for Soraya to relax and
enjoy the luxury the way Isolde could. Not
when she'd spent most of her early adult years
counting every penny and thinking they were
lucky if they had a roof over their heads for the
night. Perhaps it was jealousy, but seeing this
display of wealth didn't sit well with Soraya.
She just didn't want Raed thinking she could be
bought, or, worse, that she somehow belonged
to him simply because she'd agreed to come
out here. If he wanted someone who would be
impressed by this kind of thing and fall in line,
he'd certainly picked the wrong woman.

'You deserve to be spoiled for once. You've
spent your whole life looking after me and you
deserve someone who will do the same for you.
That definitely wasn't Frank.' They shared an
anxious giggle at the thought of Soraya's ex-
husband ever showering her with expensive
gifts.

'I should have known from our first date
when he divided the bill at the end of the meal

according to what we'd eaten and made me pay for my drinks because he'd only sipped tap water. That pretty much set the precedent for our entire marriage. That was the real Frank: selfish and petty. The rest—the apparent altruism and passion—were all for show.' Soraya did deserve someone better, but it had taken her long enough to find Frank and figure out the real man behind the façade—she didn't think she had it in her to go searching again.

'Well, maybe Raed is interested in more than your surgical skills.' Isolde waggled her eyebrows and Soraya hoped no one else could hear this conversation as they followed the royal entourage into a private function room.

'I don't think so.' Soraya tried to shut down the discussion. She didn't want to break his confidence by explaining why he might've felt indebted to her, other than trying to get her to operate on his father.

'Why else would Prince Raed have invited us?'

'Because you didn't leave him any choice?' Isolde pouted.

'You're so cynical. Why can't you just enjoy yourself for once?' Isolde grabbed her by the shoulders and gave her a playful shake.

'Why do you think?'

'Not everyone is Frank and not all men are

out to deceive you. Now, can we go and have afternoon tea with the royal family like any other normal women and stop worrying?' Isolde was grinning as she linked her arm through her sister's and they made their way over to the large table.

An older woman, dressed in the most beautiful purple silk dress embellished with gold threads, walked into the room and Raed immediately went to greet her.

'I'm glad you had some rest, Mother.' He kissed her on the cheek, as did Amir.

It was clear to Soraya that they were in the presence of the Queen, looking like the lowly commoners they were.

'I couldn't resist afternoon tea with my favourite people in the world, now, could I?' She bent down to hug Farah and Soraya felt even more as though she was intruding on private family time.

'This is Dr Soraya Yarrow, who has kindly agreed to operate on Father, and her sister, Isolde, the physiotherapist who is working with Farah.'

'Ah, ladies, my sincere gratitude for everything you're doing for my family.' She clasped her hands together and bowed her head in thanks.

'Your Majesty.' Soraya curtseyed, glad the

smart cream trouser suit she was wearing today wasn't skintight and had some give in it.

It occurred to her that she hadn't shown Raed or Amir similar respect, but she didn't recall anyone else bowing or scraping to them at work, at least not physically. There were a few members of the hospital trust she was sure did their fair share of kowtowing because they were in the presence of royalty, though Raed at least didn't seem to expect it. Guessing by their previous conversation, he probably preferred not to be reminded of his status.

Isolde attempted a curtsey too in her less forgiving leather mini dress, but the Queen gestured for her to stop. 'There's no need for formalities. You're friends of the family now, so just Djamila from now on.'

'It's so nice to meet you, Djamila.' Isolde, unrestrained by social graces now, went in for the full hug, leaving Raed's mother bemused.

'You too. Now, shall we eat?' The Queen graciously extracted herself from Isolde and gestured for her to take a seat between Farah and Amir. She sat at the head of the table, leaving Soraya to sit next to Raed.

'Thank you for the invitation.' Since they were going to be forced together during the meal, she thought it wise to attempt some sort of social niceties.

'I don't think either of us were left much option.' Although stony-faced, Raed still pulled her chair out and waited for her to be seated before he sat down.

'Thank you. You do have manners after all,' she said, the corner of her mouth tilting up into a half-smile.

Raed cocked his head to one side, a dark frown rippling across his forehead. 'Pardon me?'

Soraya flushed, knowing she'd spoken in haste. He clearly had no recollection of their previous encounter during her fundraising attempts when he'd been so rude to her. The comment had slipped out in the moment when he was being so chivalrous. A very different attitude from the one she was used to from him. Though perhaps he was on his best behaviour around his mother and it had nothing to do with her.

'You probably don't remember but we met a while ago. You…er…weren't the most welcoming colleague I had when I transferred here.' She kept her voice low as they took their seats, not wishing to embarrass him in front of his family. Everyone had their bad days when things didn't go their way work-wise, or at home. However, their line of work involved life-or-death situations, and it wasn't always easy to bounce back when things didn't go to plan.

'I'm sure I would've remembered,' he insisted.

'I was fundraising for a young carers' centre dressed in pyjamas.'

Soraya watched his memory of the incident play out across his features. His forehead evened out briefly, before furrowing again.

'Ah. Pigtails? I do remember. I was, er, going through a bad time. Another one. But that doesn't excuse my being rude to you. Sorry.' His apparent remorse over the incident redeemed him a little.

'That's okay. We all have our own troubles.' Despite her curiosity Soraya held back from asking any questions. As much as she tried to prevent her personal life leaking into her working one, it wasn't always possible. She supposed it went to prove that Raed wasn't just a surgeon born in a laboratory, he had emotions like everyone else. It was just unlucky that she'd caught him that day, and, judging by his recent behaviour, she was beginning to think he wasn't as cold-hearted as she'd assumed on first impressions.

They fell into silence as the waiters poured their tea through silver strainers into dainty china cups and brought fancy cake stands laden with goodies for them to enjoy. Once the staff left they all helped themselves to the elegant salmon-filled triangular sandwiches. Soraya had just bitten into hers when Raed shifted in his seat and leaned in to her.

'I was going through a break-up. It wasn't anything personal and I shouldn't have taken my bad mood out on you. Again, my apologies.'

She could hear the remorse in his voice, see that he meant it in those big brown eyes locked onto hers. Yet she also recognised the lingering pain behind it. Every time she spoke of her marriage breakdown it felt like a knife jabbing at her heart, reminding her that loving someone had brought her pain. It didn't matter that Frank had cheated on her, that she was better off without him, it still hurt. Though Raed seemed to have the perfect life on the outside, it was clear he was going through something similar, that someone had broken his heart too.

'It's fine.' She reached out and patted his leg in solidarity but the second she did, regret and shame flooded her entire body. It was one thing ignoring social etiquette on curtseying to a colleague, but she was pretty sure she wasn't supposed to cop a feel of his thigh muscles under the table under any circumstances.

She stopped breathing. Her face was flaming, her stomach lurching in disgust at the situation she'd put herself in. It didn't help that she'd felt him tense under her touch and they were both now staring straight ahead not knowing what to say to each other.

He almost swallowed a sandwich in one bite while studiously ignoring her. Soraya sipped her tea, wondering how the hell she was going to get out of this one, and if the fire alarm was within arm's reach. In the end she decided ignoring the incident altogether was the way to go.

She choked down part of a sandwich in an attempt to look normal and washed it down with more tea.

'I'd just been through a break-up myself so I was probably a little sensitive at the time too. We're divorced now.' Any time she said those words she cringed a little. Oversharing perhaps, but with every reinforcement of what was happening she hoped she'd come to terms with the end of her marriage.

'I'm sorry to hear that. It's never fun going through the end of a relationship. Zara and I weren't even married but it's still hard to come to terms with such a big life change. Although if we had married she might have been more inclined to stick around and support me.' He popped a whole pistachio macaron in his mouth, chewed, and swallowed it before clarifying the situation and satisfying Soraya's curiosity to some extent.

'I'm so sorry.' She resisted the urge to touch him again, even though she'd enjoyed the warm feel of his body at her fingertips. It wasn't appropriate the first time, to do it again would just be plain weird.

'Dr Yarrow, I'm sure you must be finding it surreal that we're sitting here enjoying our tea while my husband is so ill.' The Queen broke through the chatter around the table to address her directly.

'Not at all. Every family has a different way of dealing with things. It's better to carry on as normal and hope for the best, rather than congregating round his bedside night and day running yourselves into the ground waiting for news.' It was easier for the staff in that situation to get on with their jobs too, instead of having to navigate around a prematurely grieving family. There were also extra factors involved when it came to a royal family when they came with an entourage of staff and security.

'We did that the night he was admitted,' Amir added. Although he'd been relatively quiet on the journey to the hotel, Soraya had noticed he'd been engaged with Isolde as well as Farah since they'd sat down. She hoped her bubbly little sister was coaxing him out of his shell, and not overwhelming him with her personality as she was sometimes prone to do.

'Well, I saw your father this morning and, though he's not out of the woods just yet, he's holding his own. As soon as he's stable enough, I'll perform his bypass, which should get his heart back pumping as normal. He'll be in for some physical rehab after that, but I'm sure Raed and Amir have told you all of this already,' she added, addressing the Queen. These were extraordinary circumstances, not least because she was dealing with a patient whose family members were medical colleagues. Soraya couldn't help but feel under pressure to succeed under ever watchful eyes. It gave her some indication of the burden of responsibility weighing heavily on Raed's shoulders. All while dealing with the end of his relationship, and his father's ill health.

She had a new-found respect for him outside the workplace, and had never expected them to have so much in common given their very different backgrounds. Although money wasn't a factor in his struggle, she did recognise that commitment to his family, and need to protect them. No one here would ever have guessed how he'd really felt about his father's condition, or his fears about the future. She wondered if subconsciously he'd realised he'd found a kindred spirit in her and that was why he'd felt safe to express his emotions. It made a change from a man who'd kept so many things hidden from her, and it was a privilege that Raed had been able to confide in her. Perhaps not all men were only out for themselves, disregarding other people's feelings in the process, after all.

'We'll follow your advice on this one. You're in charge,' Raed said, letting Soraya know he wasn't going to give her any trouble, or interfere in his father's treatment. He trusted her judgement, and a lot more besides.

She'd been very discreet about his emotional outburst in her office, as well as understanding. He didn't know much about their family dynamics, but he was sure as the eldest sister Soraya could relate to his need to protect his family and do what was best for them. There was an inherent responsibility that a firstborn took upon their shoulders and he could see in the interactions between Soraya and Isolde that she looked out for her little sister, the way he did for his little brother.

She would've understood his need to do the right thing by stepping up to take over when it became apparent Amir couldn't, in a way Zara, an only child, never had. They both wanted what was best for their families, and would do whatever it took to make them happy. Including agreeing to this lunch. He knew Soraya didn't want to be here any more than he did but she was right, it was best to keep some sort of normality in their lives, at least for Farah, who had already suffered so much.

'Can I get that in writing?' she said, her mouth turned up at the corners.

He liked her sense of humour, and the fact she wasn't intimidated by him or his family as a whole. There were a lot of things about Soraya he apparently liked. His body had responded unexpectedly when she'd touched him earlier. The squeeze she'd given him had been an act of solidarity, he'd known that, but that awareness of her touch had wakened his weary body.

It had been a while since Zara had left and he hadn't dated since, his days too consumed by work and family issues to give space for a personal life. Perhaps this was a reminder that, despite his roles as surgeon, brother, son, and prince, he was still a man. Being alone might prevent further heartbreak, but it didn't stop that craving of a loving touch, of having someone in his life who he could just be himself with behind closed doors.

He'd noticed Soraya didn't observe royal protocol around him the way she had with his mother, especially when she'd touched him like that earlier. It was nice to think she'd forgotten his status so quickly in her hurry to comfort him, or that it had never mattered to her in the first place. She accepted who he was both in the hospital, and here with his family without judgement. Despite his prickly demeanour, which frightened most people off.

'You have my word.' He leaned in, his voice surprisingly husky, and he was sure he saw a little shiver dance across the back of her neck. It did nothing to relieve this sudden build-up of tension between them. Something that had nothing to do with their past less-than-ideal encounters, and everything to do with this new awareness of each other.

In different circumstances he might have pursued the connection they seemed to have, but there would be no room in his life for any romantic notions, even if she didn't have cause to despise him. His future was uncertain, his life here on a knife edge, and he didn't need the complication of getting attached to someone else if he had to leave.

'We do have to decide what we're going to do if the news gets out about your father. In the meantime, I think as next in line to the throne, Raed, we need to look after your security. We can't be too careful, so I've asked the security team to assign you a personal protection officer.' Raed's mother waited until everyone had enjoyed their bite-sized pastries before she tackled the issue he'd been trying to avoid for too long.

He'd been living in England for so long he hadn't had to worry about his personal security but he supposed they couldn't take the risk of something happening to him too. The prospect of having a permanent shadow didn't appeal to him, but nothing about his new position did.

'There are also some rumblings about why you and Father are spending so long here. I guess compassion has a time limit. Sorry.' Amir knocked back the rest of his tea as though it were hard liquor. Clearly he was feeling the strain of everything too.

'I think people forget we're human too. They expect we should just pack away our emotions and troubles into a neat pile and get on with our public duties. It doesn't mean we have to. None of this is on you, Amir. You and Farah concentrate on yourselves. I'll sort something out.'

He had no idea what that would be, but he didn't want Amir fretting over that too. The whole point of Raed taking over was to give his brother less to worry about. It was just another problem to add to his list of things keeping him awake at night.

It had been a rough year for all of them, but

particularly for his little brother. Sometimes Raed forgot about his feelings in all this too.

It was his father's life on the line, so soon after losing his wife, and Raed knew, even though there was no expectation for him to go home now, Amir wouldn't have simply forgotten the matter. He was someone who took his responsibilities seriously, even more than Raed. After all, he was the son who'd always towed the line and stayed out of trouble. Amir had embraced his position in the royal family, done his duty better than the eldest son who couldn't wait to spread his wings and fly away from his heritage. Not being able to fulfil his role properly now was likely eating away at Amir's conscience as much as it was Raed's.

Amir's phone buzzed, and his thunderous face when he checked the incoming message suggested it wasn't welcome news.

He held the screen up so Raed could see. 'I have an alert set up so any mention of the family online will flag up.'

'Why are our royal family living in another country?' Raed read the headline out loud and skimmed through the newspaper article, which raised the question about why the taxpayers were funding the running of the royal palace when none of the family were currently in situ. A valid concern for people who were struggling with the current cost-of-living crisis, but another potential headache for Raed.

'We're going to have to put out a statement about your father,' his mother said, her voice cracking with emotion. They all knew to be seen as fragile and vulnerable was the last thing he would want.

'Let's not rush into that just yet. At least not until he's had his operation and we know better what the situation is.' Raed wanted to put it off as long as possible to delay his return, when he'd be walking into a veritable media storm. That was something he'd rather do once he knew his family were going to be okay and he'd adapted to the idea of returning to his royal role, leaving his life in England behind for ever.

'I think it's the least we should do. We can't announce your plan to give up your right to the throne now, when there's no one else to take the reins at present. The monarchy will look more unstable than ever. I know it's not what any of us had planned but one of us has to go back to Zaki and it's going to have to be you, Raed. I have to be here for Farah.'

'I know that. I'm just asking for some more time.'

Perhaps it was selfish, people had the right to know what was going on, but he was the one who would have to deal with whatever was in store for them on their return, and it was only natural that he'd be a tad reticent about the idea of going back.

'We have to do something, Raed. The longer we leave things to fester, the harder it is going to be to recover. I still intend to go home to take up my royal duties again at some point, but in the meantime we need to give a reason for father's extended stay before there's real unrest. At the minute it's just one of the tabloids stirring up trouble. Surely there's a way to shut this down before they start speculating? Even if we're not ready to share an update on father's health, perhaps we could offer them something?' Amir tucked his phone away once everyone had had a chance to look at the article, but the reality of the situation wouldn't be as easily dismissed.

'A distraction, you mean?' In normal circumstances Raed knew they'd all be appalled by the idea of manipulating the press for their own gain, but these were extraordinary times. If it bought them some time—and whatever spin they put on the story was believed—he was all for it. Hopefully it would only be for a short while until their father was well on his way to recovery, because there was no way of knowing how long Amir and Farah were going to remain in England.

'I don't know about that…' His mother was understandably wary about any potential deception but this was to protect her too. With his father incapacitated for the foreseeable future, and Amir caring for Farah, there would be no one to look out for the Queen if Raed had to return home. And what if the worst did happen to his father and he wasn't here? For everyone's sake it would be better if they could find a way for him to stay.

'A scandal?' Isolde's eyes were wide with excitement as she clapped her hands together in glee, earning her a dirty look from her sister.

'Nothing that will damage our reputation. That's exactly what we're trying to avoid,' he reminded her. 'If the country thinks the monarchy is at risk of collapse it will have all sorts of consequences. Although we don't solely rule Zaki, and the government operates in the King's name, we are seen as a stable institution. To jeopardise that could have political implications, weaken us economically, not to mention decimate the tourist industry. We can't afford to show any sign of weakness.'

Exactly why they needed someone in situ soon.

'I do think breaking another story would buy us some time, but I'm afraid Farah and I have had more than our fair share of press coverage.' Although this was all Amir's bright idea, he was making it clear he didn't want to be the focus of 'the distraction', which came as no surprise given everything he and his daughter had been through already.

The public interest after the car accident, though understandable, had intruded on their privacy at a time when they were grieving and in pain. Raed didn't want anything to jeopardise Farah's recovery any further. Whatever plan they came up with, he knew it was going to have to be centred around him. As ever, he'd simply have to shoulder the burden for the sake of the family.

'What about a love affair?' Isolde piped up, clearly relishing being a part of this salacious discussion. Something they should really have done in private behind closed doors, but he supposed this hadn't been planned. Besides, he'd trusted Soraya not to say anything when she'd kept their earlier meeting to herself, and she'd kept his secret. He was also sure that, as the eldest sister, she'd keep Isolde in line.

'I don't think it's appropriate for us to get involved, Isolde.' As he'd predicted, Soraya took her sister to task over crossing the line and speaking out. It wasn't necessary as he doubted anyone was offended by her input, but he knew he'd have done the same thing in her position.

It was the lot of older children to try and keep their siblings in check.

'It's fine, but I don't think that's going to work, Isolde. I'm just out of a relationship and I don't think me dating again would be a big enough news story to detract from my father's whereabouts.' Even if he thought it would work, if he found someone to go along with it, he didn't think he had the energy for a romance. Fake or otherwise.

'What about a royal wedding? That would certainly grab the headlines.' Undeterred, Isolde went a step further with her romance fantasy, causing Soraya to roll her eyes in frustration.

Raed couldn't hold back this time. 'I'm not getting married just for the headlines.'

'It's not a bad idea...' Amir broke the bro code and threw him under the bus. 'You wouldn't have to actually get married, but the promise of a royal wedding and your return home to have the ceremony would certainly divert attention from Father's absence.'

'Who on earth would I even get to agree to this charade? I mean, I can't just pick a random woman off a dating site and ask her if she'd pretend to be my fiancée. Nor would I be able to trust a stranger not to go straight to the papers with the story. Even if I was up to the task, it's too much to ask of any sane person.'

'Isolde could do it!' Farah, who had been quietly taking in the adult conversation around her, was now siding with everyone else.

He could already see Isolde running through the scenario in her head, but before he could object, Amir got there first.

'No. I mean, it wouldn't be fair to ask you to do that, Isolde. You're already doing so much for our family.'

Raed didn't know if it was his imagination, or a yearning for his little brother to move on with his life after losing his wife, but he thought there was something more than a desire to keep Isolde's best interests in mind going on. Amir had been so quick to shoot down the idea, and there was the way he kept looking at her... A surge of love and optimism for his brother's future swelled in his chest, though if Amir was interested in Isolde in any way it completely ruled her out as a potential candidate for the position. Even if he was seriously considering this crazy scenario as a viable option over relocating permanently to his home country.

'No offence, Isolde, but I think you're a little on the young side. If I was looking for a bride it would be someone more my age. Someone I had things in common with. Someone like Soraya.' The room went silent as everyone turned to look at her, including Raed.

Soraya blinked in the spotlight. 'Absolutely not.'

'You'd be perfect, sis! You don't have any skeletons in your closet…well, except for an ex-husband. But you're already aware of the family circumstances,' she said to Raed. 'And it just so happens you're smart and smoking hot,' she declared, turning back to Soraya.

'It would make sense for you two to have got together, given you're work colleagues.'

Raed didn't know if Amir's endorsement of Isolde's reasoning was because he genuinely believed it was a good idea, or to get Isolde off the hook from being his prospective fake fi-ancée. Whatever it was, his idea to get Soraya involved was gaining traction. With him too. Although she was doing as much for his family as Isolde, she wasn't as much of a loose cannon, and she was already keeping his secrets.

It was becoming clear the family were looking to him to be the scapegoat. Expecting him to sacrifice his privacy to cover up what was really going on. Something he would willingly do to protect them, but circumstances were spiralling out of his control. Again.

It reminded him of those childhood days when everyone made decisions on his future for him, telling him how to behave, sending him to boarding school to mould him into the kind of person they needed him to be. He'd run away to England so he could regain that control over his own life and be the man he wanted to be. These past months had destroyed the progress he'd made, and losing Zara had made him feel like that powerless pawn again, manipulated by the royal establishment to do the right thing regardless of what he wanted.

Yet, at this present moment he didn't know how else they could get out of this mess. At least if he was faking an engagement with a fully versed participant, no one would get hurt, and once his father had recovered they could break up. No big deal. It wasn't what he had planned for his future, or something he particularly wanted to be involved in, but it would be a distraction.

If he could get Soraya to agree he would be regaining some control. It would be better to have her on side than have to fake a relationship with a stranger he'd probably have to pay for the privilege. Of course Soraya would be well compensated for her time and co-operation, but there was something less sordid about her being involved rather than an actress or stunt fiancée. They had a real connection. Okay, mostly one that had been forged over the course of twenty-four hours, but that was what made it special.

He didn't usually open himself up to anyone, trying to keep his lives as a prince and a surgeon separate, but Soraya had been different. He'd told her everything. She would understand why he had to do this, and, since she had just gone through a divorce, there'd be no risk of anyone actually developing feelings for the other. No complications, which could be a factor if they did draft in someone else and they got notions for real about becoming a princess. Until today Soraya didn't seem to have too high an opinion of him, so he doubted she was going to get carried away with some romantic fantasy of them being together. If anything, he was going to have to persuade her this was a good idea. He might even have to come with more incentive than to save his family name.

'Soraya? What do you think?'

'I think this…is crazy.' Soraya was sure the walls had begun to close in, making the room smaller and stealing the oxygen, as everyone stared at her expecting her to agree to this crazy scheme. Including her own sister, who seemed pumped up by the idea of her getting involved in something so exciting.

Pretending to be a fake fiancée to a prince

would have been right up Isolde's street. She would love the games with the press and playing up to the cameras. Isolde was the one who could pull this off, and would revel in doing so. Not that Soraya would ever have condoned it.

Soraya could see what everyone would get out of this little charade except her. Cosying up to Raed, pretending to get engaged in the eyes of the world's press, would be nothing more than a headache to her.

She wished they would all stop staring at her, hanging the weight of their expectations on her shoulders, before there was a pastel-coloured pool of vomit on the floor. The last time she'd felt this ill, as though someone were repeatedly squeezing her stomach in their fist, was when she'd discovered Frank's affair. It was the feeling of knowing her whole life was about to be upended. She'd had to make the change then for her own sake, so she didn't spend the rest of her days living with a liar and a cheat, or funding his double life. Here, she had a choice, and she was sick of always putting other people's needs before her own.

'Yes, it is, but I really don't know what else I can do other than go home and face whatever's waiting there for me. I mean, we have people running interference for us, but I'm going to have some explaining to do. It means I'll have to start getting my affairs in order here if I'm going to be leaving.'

Raed's big puppy-dog eyes weren't needed for her to feel guilty about saying no. She knew his circumstances, that he didn't want to go back, and that his family needed him here. It shouldn't be her problem.

'Is there anyone else could do this for you, Raed? If you go back now and something happens to your father—' The Queen couldn't finish the sentence, her voice breaking with emotion, clearly upset at the thought of losing her eldest's son's support.

'I don't think so, Mother. It's asking a lot from anyone who doesn't know us, or our circumstances. I—I don't even know where we would begin to set something like that up. At least with someone we trust.' He didn't look directly at Soraya, but she knew they were all thinking she was selfish in not stepping up.

The pressure to bow to everyone else's wishes was overwhelming. After Frank she'd sworn to look after only herself, and Isolde because she was an intrinsic part of who she was. This guilt, this need in her to help even when it would be detrimental to herself, was something she was still working to overcome.

'If you'll excuse me, I need to get some air.'

She pushed her chair back so quickly as she stood to leave, it toppled over.

Raed got up and repositioned her chair.

'Soraya, are you all right?' Isolde's concern was too much, bringing tears to her eyes as she tried to flee the scene.

Behind her she heard Raed say, 'I'll make sure she's okay.'

If she hadn't been so desperate to get away she would have told him not to bother coming after her. She wanted space to breathe, not have the origin of her guilt stalk her until she passed out from the pressure.

It took her a minute to navigate her way through the corridors and doors to reach the hotel lobby, and then wait impatiently for the revolving door to spit her out onto the pavement so she could actually breathe again. The sight and sounds of the busy London traffic and the smell of diesel in the air were strangely comforting, bringing her back to real life. Away from the fantasy world of fake royal romances and princes who needed rescue.

She dodged around the doorman decked out in his top hat and maroon and gold livery who'd admitted her with the family not too long ago, and walked around the corner of the hotel where she wouldn't be on display for passers-by to witness her panic attack. Bent over with her hands on her knees, she inhaled great lungsful of air.

'I'm sorry, Soraya. I know this isn't fair on you.'

She felt a hand on her back before she heard Raed's voice trying to comfort her. If she weren't so strung out from the pressure he was putting her under, she would've been touched by the concern.

'I'm your father's heart surgeon. Why is it suddenly on me to play make-believe in a royal romance to save your backside?' She knew why, she was just venting because she was cornered and needed to lash out at someone.

'I know, I know, it's ridiculous. That we're even asking you to do it shows how desperate we are. Maybe I should take Isolde up on her offer…' Hands in his pockets and staring down at his shoes, he looked dejected, but she had to remain strong. Folding at the first sign of vulnerability was not how the new Soraya was going to be able to move on with her life. Away from men who took advantage of her.

Yet she didn't want Isolde to be in the line of fire either. She'd just gone through a messy break-up and didn't need another complication in her life right now. Isolde was impetuous, jumping into relationships, and situations, that weren't always good for her. All that attention and pressure wouldn't be good for her mental health at a time when she was particularly vulnerable. Soraya knew herself the effect a break-up could have and didn't want her little sister to get hurt all over again if all of this was to fall apart and her life got picked over in the press. Sometimes Isolde didn't know what was best for her.

'No. Leave her out of this.'

'She volunteered, Soraya, and I'm all out of options if you won't help.'

'She's been through enough and there isn't anything in it for her, or me, that would justify opening up our private lives to be scrutinised by the whole world. We both know that's what will happen for any future wife of a prince.'

'So, you want money, is that what you're saying?' Raed's face was dark, his pleading eyes now filled with contempt that Soraya knew she didn't deserve.

'No. I'm saying I see the benefits for you and your family in all of this, but for me or Isolde it's asking for trouble. Especially if anyone finds out it's all an act.' She could only imagine the fallout if it was discovered the 'engagement' had been a cover for his father's illness, and an excuse to keep Raed from taking up his rightful place at home. There was a lot at stake for them all, but more for the royal family to gain than for her and Isolde.

Raed nodded, as though he was giving serious consideration to what she was saying. 'We're all hoping it won't come to that, but I understand that you'd be taking all the risk for no reward in this scenario.'

'That's not what—'

'What if we made a considerable donation to your charity? Enough to fund that centre you wanted to set up.' Raed interrupted her denial that she was in this for any kind of payoff with an incentive that made her reconsider that notion.

She'd struggled to raise the money she'd wanted for the charity, to give young carers a place to hang out to get a reprieve from the intense home life she'd had to endure as a young teen. With some extra funding she hoped to have enough to even pay for a counsellor who could provide a listening ear to those children forced to grow up too quickly under the burden of responsibility.

'I...er...' It was tempting. Although she would be putting the needs of others over her own comfort once more, it would be for a good cause. It would be giving young carers somewhere they could be with other children their own age, who understood what they were going through, a safe space where they could simply be kids. If she could give other families that respite, that comfort of knowing they weren't alone, that she'd never known, it would be worth it.

'Please, Soraya. We need your help.' Raed's plea, coupled with the chance to make a real difference to children weighed down by responsibility of caring for their families, wore away the last of her resolve.

'Okay, okay. I'll do it,' she huffed out on a sigh. 'I guess I'm going to have to pucker up and play nice with my beloved Prince Raed.' She clasped her hands to her heart in an exaggerated swoon, while inside it really was beating a tattoo fast enough to make her faint at the thought of being Raed's pretend lover.

Raed gathered her in an uncharacteristically enthusiastic hug. 'Thank you, so much.'

Soraya let herself be swept up into his strong arms. She'd forgotten how nice it was to be pressed close to a warm, male body. That solid reassurance of a wall of muscle against her was something she missed, along with that feeling of security. Even if none of it had been real with Frank.

She inhaled the masculine scent of him and sighed. The smile on her face as she let him hold her for a fraction longer than a celebratory hug would normally necessitate told Soraya she was doomed.

CHAPTER THREE

'I'LL HAVE HIM back to you as soon as possible,' Soraya promised as they wheeled Raed's father away to prep for surgery.

'He's in the best hands, Mother.' Raed comforted Djamila, who was crying into his shoulder. He gave Soraya a smile and a nod, as if to say, 'I know you've got this.'

She swallowed hard, hoping for all their sakes that she had.

The family, including the King, knew exactly what was going to happen. She'd talked them through the entire procedure so there wouldn't be any surprises; hopefully that went for her too. Surgery, and heart surgery in particular, always carried risks. Even the general anaesthetic used to put the King to sleep came with warnings. As heart operations went, it was a standard procedure she carried out regularly, but that didn't mean there wasn't the possibility of complications. The surgical team always had to be ready in case everything didn't go to plan, but her patient seemed in good overall health, apart from his heart, so it should go smoothly.

She would be lying if she said she wasn't nervous as she made the first incision. The responsibility of having his life in her hands wasn't lost on her.

'Okay, let's do this,' she said to herself as much as to the rest of the team.

It was more pressure than usual knowing they had a king under the knife, even though they were using off-pump coronary bypass surgery. A relatively new procedure, which, although it took less time than the conventional methods, meant less chance of bleeding during surgery. It also had increased recovery times, and was more technically demanding. She had to graft vessels while the heart was still beating. With two coronary blood vessels narrowed, Soraya had to attach two new grafts to divert the blood supply around the blocked artery. Something that always had her holding her breath until they knew everything was working as it should. Not every heart surgeon had the training to use this method and she supposed it was part of the reason Raed had chosen her to perform the surgery on his father.

Today in particular she was relieved to see and hear the heart beating of its own accord.

As she fixed the breastbone back together using metal wires, and sewed the skin on the chest back together, all she could think of was Raed and the relief he would feel.

The hours waiting for his father to come out of surgery seemed to drag on, every second ticking by noted by the loud wall clock in the family waiting room.

'Raed, you're making a mess.' Despite all attempts to get his mother to leave, she'd insisted on waiting with him and Amir until they knew his father was out of surgery and safe.

He looked down and noticed the pile of paper snow at his feet where he'd been subconsciously shredding the takeaway cup in his hands.

'Sorry.' He scooped up the debris from his anxious wait and dumped it in the recycling bin.

Although Soraya would be feeling under pressure performing the life-or-death operation, time seemed to go quicker inside that operating theatre. It was so much harder, emotionally, to be on this side of the patient-surgeon divide.

Lately he felt as though he were falling apart just like that cup he'd decimated. For years he'd done his own thing, been in charge of his own life, and within a few months it had all been ripped away. That loss of control had clearly impacted him when he was finding it so much more difficult to keep a lid on his feelings. Especially around Soraya.

Even yesterday, hugging her out of relief for agreeing to help was out of character for him. Something he regretted, not only because it represented another display of emotion he should have kept at bay, but also because now he had the memory of holding her in his arms to contend with. Remembering the warmth of her body pressed against his wasn't going to help matters when they were going to be forced together for this fake engagement debacle. It needed to be a clinical transaction with no further emotional complications if he was going to get through it. He did not have time or room in his life for anything more at present.

When the door opened, his own heart felt as though it had stopped, ready to hear the news that could affect the rest of his life. He'd never been so pleased to see Soraya as she walked in with a smile.

'Mr Ayad is out of surgery and on the recovery ward. Everything went as planned but we'll have to keep him under close observation for the next forty-eight hours in intensive care just to make sure there are no complications. He should be able to be discharged in about a

week or so, with full recovery usually taking
about twelve weeks.'

Raed knew there was a risk of stroke after a
heart operation like this, but he was also aware
his father had survived the surgery and was in
the best place should anything untoward arise.

'Thank you so much, Dr Yarrow.' His mother
let out a sob, probably the same relief they were
all feeling.

'You're welcome,' Soraya said, and he could
see her eyes welling up, as though the enor-
mity of the situation had finally hit her too.
After all, she'd been dragged into their family
drama beyond his father's medical needs, and
she would likely be glad when her role in all
of this was over.

Amir shook her hand first and it looked to
Raed as though he was fighting to hold back
the tears too. Raed still felt a little too numb
but he was sure it would hit him later, in private. He'd already shown too much of himself
in front of Soraya. It had surprised him as much
as her that he'd opened himself up to her about
his personal turmoil, begging for her help twice
in the space of a couple of days.

Soraya had just happened to be in the wrong
place at the wrong time, twice, to witness him
fall apart. Or perhaps he recognised something
in her that made him feel safe sharing his fears

and asking for her help. Whatever the cause, he knew he had to stop doing it.

'Thank you, Soraya, for everything.' He moved in for a handshake next, but it seemed so inadequate given everything she'd done for them. With a tug of her hand, he pulled her in closer for a hug.

Okay, so maybe one more display would be forgiven in the circumstances.

If this were any other surgeon it might have been inappropriate, but as she hugged him back he knew they'd both needed this. In a way, she'd been under as much pressure as he had to save the family and his country.

The soft comfort of her body pressed against his was something he could have luxuriated in if they'd been in private, and she'd let him; he needed it. But he was aware they weren't alone. He reluctantly let go.

'You don't know how much this means.'

'I do,' she replied, and the flush of pink in her cheeks and her dilated pupils said she wasn't just talking about his father's successful surgery.

A surge of awareness reinvigorated his weary body as he looked into those beautiful big blue eyes, and a sudden need to kiss her came from nowhere.

Raed took a step back. He knew this had

to be a reaction to her saving his father's life, saving him from having his own turned upside down in the blink of an eye. Because he wasn't ready for anything more.

Soraya rang the buzzer for Raed's apartment. It was on the top floor, of course, part of a swanky new complex down by the Thames with river views and transport links on the doorstep. All angles and glass, it wasn't exactly what she would describe as pretty but was certainly expensive.

'Come up,' he commanded over the intercom as the door slowly swung open.

The air-conditioned lobby and bank of elevators wildly contrasted with the graffiti-decorated hallway of Isolde's building, which often smelled so bad Soraya had to cover her nose until she reached the flat.

As the lift rose, her stomach dropped. She had no reason to be nervous. This wasn't a booty call or anything untoward at all. Unless you included conspiring to defraud the public over an alleged romance in that bracket. Raed had simply suggested she come to his place to talk about the terms of their arrangement in private, away from listening ears at the hospital.

Perhaps it was the prospect of being truly alone with him that was making her palms sweat and her pulse race. Although that didn't explain why, when he'd hugged her at the hospital, her body had gone into meltdown. She'd put it down to exhaustion at the time after the stress of performing a successful surgery on the King. That was the only reason she'd agreed to come here tonight, telling herself it had simply been a momentary need for some comfort of her own.

After everything she'd been through with Frank there was no room in her life for silly crushes, especially on a man so burdened with his own problems and responsibilities. If she ever intended to share her life with another man, it would have to be with someone who put her needs first for a change. She was done being a doormat and the only reason she'd agreed to partake in this charade was because she felt sorry for him.

Although when Soraya saw Raed leaning in his doorway and her heart gave an extra beat, she considered for a moment that this was more than sympathy.

'Thanks for coming,' he said, pushing the door open further so she could step inside.

'Well, we have a few things to sort out.' She took a deep breath before entering, feeling as though she were walking into the lion's den.

The apartment was spacious, sleek and masculine, just like Raed. The pristine leather sofa looked as though it had never been sat on, the chrome in the kitchen area shining so bright she doubted it had ever been used. The place had all the hallmarks of a busy surgeon, and warning signs of a man who had no time for a personal life. Probably why his girlfriend had left him when it had become clear he'd have more responsibilities in his home country too.

'Take a seat,' he instructed. 'Can I get you a drink?'

'No, thanks. This isn't a social call, remember?' The reminder was as much for her as for Raed. As soon as they'd discussed the terms, she was out of here.

His face darkened, the smile fading as he took a seat opposite her. 'Of course. Now my father is successfully through surgery—thanks to you—I hope it won't be long before he can return to the throne. However, we will still have to distract the press in the meantime.'

'That's where I come in.' It wasn't a position she'd ever imagined herself in, as a decoy for a royal family to avoid scandal. Nor was it one she relished, but she'd agreed to do it to help the family and get funding for the centre so she had to go along with whatever Raed had planned. Within reason.

'We will have to announce our engagement.'

He paused as though waiting for her to react, and, though she baulked inwardly, it wasn't a surprise.

'Okay. Then what?' Soraya was sure it wouldn't be as easy to get rid of the press interest by simply taking out a newspaper ad. She had no idea how invested the English tabloids were in the Zaki royal family in general, or if news would even filter back to his home country to justify the lie.

Raed cleared his throat then studiously stared at his feet and she just knew she wasn't going to like what came next.

'I'm going to have to take a leave of absence from work and go back to Zaki. Temporarily.' He took a deep breath. 'I need you to come with me.'

Soraya opened her mouth to object, then swallowed the *No!* she wanted to bellow. It was only natural he'd expect a fiancée to return to his home country with him if he was going to announce his betrothal. However, the idea of a trip away with Raed unnerved her when she apparently couldn't even spend an evening in his presence without fretting over the implications.

She sat for a moment before she spoke.

'Is there no other way? I've got work to think about.' It was more than her responsibilities at home that worried her, but she doubted that confiding in Raed about her body's inappropriate responses to being near him was going to do either of them any good.

He shook his head. 'Trust me, I've been going over every scenario in my head. I don't want to spend any longer out there than necessary, but I think if we're going to convince everyone that we're a couple, that the monarchy is as strong as ever, we need to put on a united public front.'

'I'd hate to leave Isolde—'

'She isn't a child, Soraya,' he interrupted, making her bristle.

'I know that, but she is my responsibility. I'm sure you can appreciate I can't just walk away and forget about her. I live with her and pay half the rent so it's only natural that I would have concerns about leaving her to travel halfway across the world.' She didn't like being called out like that. Okay, so she was a tad overprotective but that wasn't such a bad thing when her little sister was the only family she had left. Raed certainly didn't have any right to tell her how to feel when she was doing him a favour.

He raised his eyebrows at her sharp retort, but at least had the sense not to criticise her decision any further. 'It would only be for a few days.'

'What do I have to do?' Now he'd got her

back up, her arms were folded, telling him he was going to have to work harder to impress her if he wanted her to play ball.

'There's an event soon that my father usually attends. I thought if we at least made an appearance there, to coincide with the engagement announcement, perhaps you might only be required to stay for a few days. I'll remain in Zaki until my parents are able to travel, but we can say you have to return home to get your affairs in order before the wedding. I can cover your rent with Isolde and have someone check in on her if you need.'

Okay, he was trying. A few days was as good as she could hope for in the circumstances. Though she doubted it was going to be the most relaxing time off she'd ever had. Apart from her unwanted apparent attraction to Raed, and the stress of faking an engagement to a prince in his home country, there was also the matter of Raed himself. He'd made no attempt to disguise the fact he was ill at ease with this part of his life and she could only imagine his mood to be darker than ever once he was forced to live it indefinitely.

'I don't think that's needed, but thank you. What about you? Weren't you set to announce you relinquish your official position in the royal family?'

He shrugged. 'There's no chance of doing that now. Amir insists he still wants to return some day, but my father's health has given me a wake-up call. I can't hide from my responsibility for ever. Other than my job, I have no real ties in London. It makes sense for me to return on a more permanent basis instead of Amir when Farah is making progress here.'

'That's not fair on you.' It was silly, but Soraya had felt as though she'd been slapped across the face when he'd said he had nothing to stay in the country for. She had no claim on Raed, indeed she didn't wish for one. For him to move abroad indefinitely should relieve her of a lot of her current stress. Yet seeing him so despondent over a future he apparently had no control over brought an inexplicable sadness that she wasn't going to be a part of it. Even when he sometimes lived up to that cool reputation that set her on edge.

'Since when is life fair?' His scowl softened into a smile and Soraya's heart gave another skip of happiness at witnessing the transformation. It was those moments when he let his defences drop and show a glimpse of the man behind the carefully groomed exterior that caught her off guard and gave her reason to like him.

If there were any cause for him to abandon

his dark and brooding façade on their trip away together, she considered herself in big trouble with no way of avoiding it. At least tonight she could go back to the flat, put some distance between them, and talk some sense into herself. Faking a role as his fiancée in his home country wasn't going to leave room for an escape from these unwanted feelings she was beginning to have towards him.

'Well, let me know the arrangements so I can get some time off.' Soraya rushed to get to her feet, desperate to get away for now.

Raed saw her to the door despite her protest that she could let herself out.

'Thanks again for doing this, Soraya. I don't know what I'd do without you at the minute.'

The last thing she saw before turning away was that beautiful smile again. She might need a drink tonight after all.

'Once we've seen Father and said our goodbyes we can head to the airport.' Raed wasn't in a particular hurry to get on that plane but at least with Soraya by his side he'd have some sense of normalcy. Since his father had pulled through those first critical forty eight hours, the family had agreed it was time for Raed to return to Zaki.

'Yay,' she said, with a distinct lack of enthusiasm.

He was grateful she'd agreed to go with him when she had no real obligation to travel outside the country. It was one thing pretending to be a couple in her home town, but it was a huge favour she was doing him by continuing the pretence overseas. He could probably have fronted it out on his own, made some excuse later as to why his fiancée hadn't accompanied him, but he would be glad of an ally who would treat him as Raed, instead of a prince.

There was no need to hide his true self around Soraya, although he could do with keeping a tighter hold of his emotions around her. At least by bringing her along he felt as though he had some control over what was happening. Despite the burgeoning feelings he was having towards her. He hoped, since they would only be together for a few days and busy with public engagements, he wouldn't have the time or inclination to explore them any further. Given the circumstances it would be pointless anyway. They were going to be living in two different countries, both concentrating on the welfare of their own families, with their personal lives on hold.

'I know it's a hardship being around me, but it won't be for long. I promise.' After her swift exit from his apartment three nights ago it was obvious she didn't want to spend any more time with him than was absolutely necessary. Which made her decision to travel back to Zaki all the more surprising. He supposed that funding meant more to her than he'd realised.

'Well, I've managed this car journey with you so hopefully I'll survive a little longer,' Soraya said with a heavy dose of sarcasm.

'If you could pretend you like me, that would probably help too.' Raed knew that the only quick solution to detract attention away from his father's ill health was to let the press and the public believe they were together, and Soraya was simply a colleague that he had fallen for at the hospital. Except it entailed spending more time with her, something that was already proving detrimental to his health when his sleep had been disrupted since the moment his father had taken ill.

He knew he wasn't her favourite person either, given he'd been unforgivably rude to her on their first meeting, and especially now, after he'd emotionally blackmailed her into helping with this charade.

Although his resolve had considerably weakened when she'd been a listening ear, showing compassion when he'd inadvertently opened up about his struggles, he was too wounded, too raw from the end of his relationship to contemplate another. Even though he was becoming increasingly attracted to the woman tasked with saving his father's life and the country's future.

If Zara, the woman he'd thought he would spend the rest of his life with, couldn't handle the idea of being part of the royal family, it was a wasted exercise expecting anyone else to want that lifestyle either. Especially someone who was only in his life temporarily. Who had a successful career she would never give up for the responsibility his family demanded. He knew, not only because Zara hadn't wanted to do it, but also because neither did he. Once his father was out of the woods they would end things because Soraya Yarrow was not a woman he should be getting close to. At least not emotionally. He no longer had a choice over the physical distance when their closeness was a necessity to maintain their cover.

'We're going to have to put on a bit of a show when we get out of this car,' he reminded her as they pulled up outside the hospital.

'I know.' Her grimace didn't do much for his ego.

'I don't want to do this any more than you do, Soraya. Trust me. I have more important things to concentrate on than this ridiculous farce.'

'I think you might need to take some acting classes if you think calling me a ridiculous farce is going to persuade anyone we're a couple, including me.' Soraya huffed out of the car before he had a chance to apologise and explain it wasn't anything personal.

'Wait, Soraya—' He had to hustle to catch up with her across the car park and when he tried to put his arm around her shoulder she almost shrugged him off.

'Hey, we have to do this,' he reminded her. 'You can shower straight after if you need to, but for now we need to convince everyone that this is real.'

Raed saw the resistance in her eyes, felt it in the tension of her body, but at least she let him touch her without punching him in the face.

'How do we even know there's anyone watching?' she asked, looking around as though expecting to see long-lens cameras pointing at her from every direction.

'There might have been a tip-off that the Prince drops off his new girlfriend at work every morning. We thought it would make it more believable to see us together before we make our surprise announcement.'

'You actually set this up?' She stopped walking and turned to look at him, her blue eyes blazing with indignation at the tactics they'd used to set their plan in motion.

'Not personally. We have advisers and press officers who deal with this sort of thing. I know it seems underhanded but public figures and celebrities do it all the time when they want to promote something or get attention. Our circumstances are different, but we need to get this story out there to replace the truth. Time is of the essence.'

He sighed and reached out a hand to take hers. This time she didn't try to pull away from him. 'The lies don't sit well with me either. Goodness knows I've told enough over the years to hide my real identity, and learned my lesson the hard way that the truth always comes out in the end. But in this instance we're just hoping by the time it all comes out Father will be recovered and any crisis averted. Don't hate me for this, Soraya.'

Her features softened as she listened to his explanation of why they were doing this. 'I don't hate you, Raed. Neither of us asked to be in this position. Well, technically you did, but I know that was because you were desperate. I understand. You love your family and your country, just as I love my sister and would do anything for her. It's a cross eldest children have to bear, I guess.'

In an act of what he assumed was solidarity, and perhaps for the cameras, Soraya laced her fingers through his and leaned into him as they walked into the hospital. For a brief moment Raed wished it weren't just an act, that he'd met someone who understood his position and was reconciled with it. Who loved him enough that they would want to be with him whatever happened. Something he'd never had in his life from his parents or a partner.

He wished that Soraya weren't someone else who would walk away when the going got tough and leave him to pick up the pieces of his broken heart again.

But the only thing more dangerous than getting caught in a lie was believing it himself.

'How are you feeling today, Your Majesty?' Although Soraya and Raed were leaving for the airport, they'd both wanted to check in on her patient first. After a meeting with the night staff, it seemed he was recovering as well as could be expected, even if he still looked fragile lying on the hospital bed, plugged into all the machines monitoring his vital signs.

'As though I've been trampled by a herd of wild horses,' he said weakly.

Soraya didn't know the man that well beyond their doctor-patient relationship, but she appreciated his sense of humour. It showed a strength of character. His son displayed a similar stubbornness when it came to survival.

'It's not surprising after what you've gone through, Father, but you're here and that's all that matters.' This was a softer side of Raed she was seeing as he moved to his father's bedside.

Soraya wondered how long it would be before the shutters came down again. There were flashes of kindness and compassion in Raed, but they were quickly overshadowed by the dark brooding introspection he seemed to lose himself in occasionally too. It was little wonder when his life was so complicated, but it made it difficult to get to know the real Raed, which was probably just as well when her body betrayed her every time he touched her. She knew it was all for the cameras, but the goosebumps along her skin were proof she was refusing to believe it deep down.

'I know you're still in some discomfort and we'll give you some painkillers to help with that, but we will have to get you mobile as soon as possible. Tomorrow we will look at moving you from the bed into a chair at least. The physiotherapist will also work with you on some exercises to keep your muscles supple and an occupational therapist can help prepare you to undertake daily tasks again.'

'No rest for the wicked, eh?' he joked to a stony-faced Raed.

'It's all for your own benefit, Father.'

The King tutted. 'For yours too. The sooner I take my place again, the quicker you're off the hook.'

'I'm going back to Zaki now until you're better.'

'You can't blame me for that, Raed. It's not my fault you were living a lie. If you'd just stayed at home and done your duty in the first place—'

'Okay, I don't think this is the right time or place to debate that. Your father needs to rest, he doesn't need any stress right now.' She didn't know anything about their relationship but from this brief interaction it was obvious things were strained between them. Although, given everything Raed had done to try and protect his family, it was clear he loved his father, even if he didn't like to show it. It was safe to say those shutters had slammed down again as soon as he knew his father was out of immediate danger.

'It's probably better if I go, in that case. I'm glad you're on the way to recovery, Father. It's all any of us want.' To his credit Raed didn't relay the details of their newly formed fake romance, or indeed the fact that the paparazzi were sniffing around looking for a story. That would have given the King a lot to worry about and might have hindered his recovery. Yet another sign that Raed cared about his father more than he probably even realised.

She recognised well that need to keep problems secret so as not to upset family members, given she'd been doing it her whole life. The trouble was that the person holding the secrets, dealing with the problems, was often the one who needed the most support, and no one knew it.

'We'll let you get some rest for now, Your Majesty. I just need to need to see Isolde, then we can go, Raed.' The majority of her work had been done in the operating theatre and her colleagues would be on hand should any complications arise, making sure her royal patient progressed as well as he should.

'Can I have visitors? I would like to see my wife.' The King looked small as he made the plea and it was hard for Soraya to picture him in all of his regal finery ruling a country. She could only imagine how difficult it was for Raed to see him in this light. Perhaps that unstable mood had something to do with the uncertainty still remaining around his parent's health, and therefore his own future.

'Of course. I know the Queen is keen to see

you, too.' It was nice to see a smile on the elderly man's face. He was no doubt afraid about what was going to happen to him and needed the comfort and support of his wife. It was a refreshing change to see a couple who still genuinely cared for one another, given that Frank had turned to someone else for that and ended their marriage.

In the past few days she'd got to know them a little, and liked them a lot. She wanted to protect them from any further heartache, but for that to happen she was going to have to keep this charade with Raed going for a while longer at least. It was one more sacrifice on her part in order to fulfil someone else's needs—and an ongoing battle to maintain her peace of mind. That need for self-preservation since her marriage break-up was screaming so loud for her to find something else to do, somewhere else to be, it was deafening.

For now she had to stick her fingers in her ears and pretend she couldn't hear it.

CHAPTER FOUR

'THIS COULD BE part of a ransom plot, you know.'

'Hmm?' Raed barely registered Soraya's murmurings, his head buried in his phone, while she watched the world beneath them come to life.

After saying goodbye to Isolde, making sure the freezer was full of home-cooked dinners, and there was no washing left in the machine to go mouldy in her absence, Soraya had joined Raed and flown out overnight. Though her travelling companion seemed to have spent most of their journey arranging his schedule. Eventually she'd given up trying to hold a conversation with him and dozed as long as the mid-air turbulence had let her. Shaken violently awake, fear gripping her heart, she'd decided this stunt was more like something Isolde would have done—spontaneous and exciting. Unlike her, who had been the responsible, sensible one of the pair her whole life. She wasn't enjoying the experience so far, despite their attentive steward.

'Flying out on a private jet with a prince sounds like the elaborate plot of a Liam Neeson movie, or an Isolde whim. It does not seem the sort of rational decision an older, more responsible sister would usually make,' she mused aloud for Raed's benefit, not that he seemed to be listening.

With her head pressed up against the aeroplane window, the small island kingdom that was about to become her temporary new home gradually came into view. The palm trees and turquoise seas were a far cry from the bustling city of London she was used to. Slowly, signs of life filtered through the gloomy morning mist. The coloured lights from moving vehicles snaked their way through the hills, like arteries pumping life into the city that was splayed out before them now. The lights and movement of the traffic heralding the start of the day as the sun rose in the sky outside the window, burning away the darkness to replace it with the bright display of dawn emerging.

Now, as they came in to land in this unknown terrain, Soraya was experiencing a flurry of doubts suddenly bombarding her about what she was doing. They were in a foreign country, at Raed's mercy. The nervous energy that usually fuelled her through tricky life-changing operations was mixed with a sense of foreboding.

'Could you buckle your seat belts in preparation for landing? Thank you.' The lovely steward who had been looking after them on the flight, supplying a seemingly endless supply of drinks, snacks, blankets and pyjamas, supervised their compliance before taking his own seat.

As they touched down Soraya was afraid that bump when they hit the tarmac was the same moment she'd come back to earth and realise she'd been lured out into the middle of the ocean under false pretences. Any second now she'd be bundled into a waiting car and trafficked over the border never to be heard from again. Except Raed stood to gain more from her as a fake fiancée than a kidnap victim.

The door opened but Soraya remained in her seat just a fraction longer, waiting for masked strangers to burst onboard and prove her fears right. It didn't happen.

As they climbed down the steps she could see several suited men waiting below with a black limousine to collect them. She almost turned back.

'Good morning, Your Royal Highness. It's good to have you home.'

Raed nodded an acknowledgement to the smallest of the men who'd stepped forward to greet them. Soraya wondered if the other silent, intimidating members of the group were security detail. It was a little unnerving to think they needed this level of protection when they'd just set foot in the country, but she supposed no one wanted to take any chances with their safety and for that she was grateful. If there was a risk that someone thought them potential targets, whether for political or financial gain, it was preferable to have multiple bodyguards whose bodies were so pumped up they looked as though they would burst out of those tailored black suits at any moment.

'What about our bags?' She didn't have much in the world but what she did have was packed into her luggage and she wasn't mentally prepared to lose anything else.

One of the burly squad stepped forward. 'We'll take care of it.'

She didn't dare argue with him and climbed into the back seat of the limo with Raed, phone in hand to text Isolde the second she had a signal.

Landed safely. On way to the palace. Don't forget to leave the bins out. x

'It's only been a matter of hours.' Raed was peering over her shoulder at the text.

Soraya hastily shoved her phone back in her bag. 'Yes, well, she's not used to doing everything herself.'

'What did she do when you were married and living in a different house?' He grinned at her, and though she was glad to see he was relaxing a bit more, he was highlighting the part of her personality that both she and Isolde were struggling with.

'She had a partner then too to help with things.' Since leaving Frank she'd busied herself in her sister's life, taking up where she'd left off before she got married. Perhaps it was because she needed to be needed again, she'd replaced caring for her husband for looking after Isolde. There were times that Isolde got exasperated by her constant cleaning and fussing, but Soraya had to keep busy, make herself useful around the place. She was lucky her sister had agreed to let her stay in the flat, because, without her, Soraya had nothing and no place to go.

'You do too much,' he said gently.

'Says you,' she childishly bit back, knowing everything he said was true.

They sat in silence for the remainder of the journey but thankfully they seemed to fly through the traffic, the driver expertly weaving in and out of lanes, all the while being followed by another car containing the security team. It wasn't long before they were driving up the impressive mall towards the palace. Once they'd entered the grounds through the large ornate golden gates, Soraya wound down the window to take it all in.

The air was warm on her face, the sun now making its presence known, the golden spires of the palace glinting in the light. The white, gold and cobalt-blue columns and arches were imposing in the vast green landscape, and the opulent, extravagant exterior of the sprawling palace couldn't have contrasted more with her humble upbringing. She wondered which part of the building housed the dungeon for stupid Englishwomen who agreed to fake a relationship with the Prince.

Before she had time to panic any more, the door opened and a hand came in to help her out of the car. The guard walked them into the palace then seemed to disappear, leaving her to marvel at the décor in the massive hall.

Soraya spun around on the white marble floor, staring at the ceiling. 'Wow. It's like something out of a fantasy novel.'

She was captivated by the bright colour of the rich royal-blue mosaic inlays covering every inch of the walls and the ornate stained-glass windows above multiple archways. It was all too much, yet breathtaking at the same time.

'I'm glad my home meets with your approval.' Raed's deep, authoritative voice echoed around the walls.

'It's stunning.'

'I'll have someone show you to your room. I have some business to attend to, if you'd like to freshen up before our outing.' This efficient, closed Raed, checking his watch and effectively abandoning her in a foreign country, was completely different from the man who'd begged for help in her office less than a week ago. It was probably her fault he'd reverted after she'd called him out for taking on too much in the name of his family too.

She decided she preferred the man who hadn't been afraid to take her into his confidence, sharing his fears, instead of blocking her out.

'I'm not sure I have anything suitable to wear to this…event,' she whispered, feeling even more out of place now she could see the luxury he'd grown up in. Although she'd brought her best clothes, she didn't want to make a spectacle of herself if she didn't measure up as a suitable match for Zaki's prince.

'It doesn't matter. You're here to do a job, not to impress anyone with your wardrobe.'

'Just wave, smile, and hang on your arm,' she said with sickly sweet sarcasm.

'Exactly,' he confirmed before turning away, oblivious to her obvious discomfort. Or perhaps he simply didn't care.

The thought that she really was nothing more to him than a convenient cover story stung more than it should.

'My generous benefactor.' Soraya curtseyed as Raed met her in the magnificent hallway, wearing the beautiful outfit that had mysteriously appeared in her room not long after she'd voiced her anxiety about her wardrobe.

When she'd finally emerged from the sumptuous tub in her bathroom, the air thick with steam and essential oils, an extravagant red and gold gown had been laid out across her bed. Clearly, Raed had been listening after all.

'I didn't want you to feel uncomfortable.'

'Or perhaps you were afraid I'd embarrass you by turning up in my civvies?' she suggested.

Raed laughed. 'So sceptical.'

The only reason she held onto her cynicism was she was pretty sure he could coerce her into doing anything with one hangdog look. Soraya shuddered, realising the situation she'd put herself in, where she was at his mercy because she didn't want to let anyone down. Since Frank she'd learned to be more cautious about giving her trust so easily.

'I've had to be. My ex-husband lied to me and ruined my life. Remember I'm only doing this because there are people relying on me.' She hadn't meant to share such deeply personal information—it was humiliating—but she needed him to understand she couldn't simply blindly follow wherever he led. Frank had left her with serious scars and she'd been married to him for a decade. She'd be a fool to trust a man who clearly had an agenda other than her welfare.

'I'm sorry. Although I had convinced myself it was my stunning personality that had been the enticement.'

She rolled her eyes at his attempt to lighten the mood, although she was glad to have another glimpse of the Raed she'd come to know. 'Obviously it was the idea of faking a relationship with the Crown Prince that I couldn't resist.'

'Obviously.' He was grinning at her and she couldn't help but return it, regardless that she was still a little mad at him for hijacking her. She liked that she could make him crack that ever-present frown and smile once in a while.

'You haven't told me where we're going. I would like to know so I can stop fretting about what it is I'm getting into, or, you know, worry more that I'm not up to whatever task is expected of me.' The more she talked about her anxiety, the quicker her breathing became, until she was making herself dizzy with the lack of oxygen.

'Of course. I didn't mean to panic you. For this story to work we need to raise our profile, so I thought we needed a more public setting.'

Soraya appreciated the explanation, but he still hadn't told her where, or what they'd be doing.

As if reading her mind, Raed continued. 'It's nothing to worry about, honest. We will be merely spectating. It's a horse show with international participants competing in different equestrian disciplines. Father is well known for his love of horses and was invited as a guest of honour. I'm going to be taking his place awarding the prizes at the end, but you don't have to take part in that. I simply need you to sit next to me and, when you're not watching the horses, look at me adoringly.'

'Raed, I know nothing about horses.'

'Soraya, neither do I.'

At least by the time they arrived at the arena, they'd forged a new bond other than their resentment of being forced together, and their newly single relationship status.

'Oh, yeah, I hope red's your colour,' Raed whispered into her ear as they exited the car onto the carpeted walkway rolled out specially to welcome their visit.

Soraya wasn't prepared for the rush of noise that greeted her outside. She stumbled back as a crowd gathered near the entrance surged forward, cameras snapping and people shouting for their attention.

'You're okay, I've got you.' Raed put his arm around her waist, steadying her on her feet and guiding her towards the building.

Once she was safe in the knowledge that he would keep her upright, and with the security team pushing the crowd back, Soraya could breathe again. They were whipped through the building into a private lift away from the general public and taken to a private box to view the event from on high.

'I didn't realise you're so popular.'

'Not usually, but I think my return has stirred up interest.'

'It's like having a fast pass at an amusement park, except you're able to bypass people everywhere to get to the head of the queue.' Soraya marvelled at the perks that came with this privileged lifestyle. After spending a lifetime working to support her younger sister and doing all the worrying for two, it would be nice to have people who did things for her for once.

Raed fixed her with his dark stare, but this time he had a twinkle in his eye. 'We don't have to queue.'

He broke into a big cheesy grin that couldn't fail to make her laugh, just as the catering staff came in to offer them trays of champagne and canapés. She helped herself to a glass of bubbles and some smoked salmon.

'Sorry, I was hungry.' She wasn't sure why she felt the absurd need to apologise. Perhaps because often, when at fancy medical functions laden with lavish spreads, she'd been given the impression it was bad etiquette to actually eat the food.

'Can I get you anything else? I'm sure the chef would be happy to accommodate you. Some beans on toast or a full English breakfast, perhaps?' He was teasing but Soraya's stomach was grumbling and, as lovely as the food seemed, it was rich compared to the plain meals she was used to cooking at home.

'Thank you, but I'm sure this will suffice for now.' She said it as much to the waiter as Raed—he was hovering beside her as though he was expecting her to plant herself face first into the serving platter to scoff the lot.

Raed whispered something to him before he left. Likely an apology for bringing an unexpected plus one to gatecrash the party.

She wandered out onto the balcony to see what the view was like, only to be met with cheers and a wall of camera phones facing towards her. A hand grabbed her and pulled her back inside.

'I should have warned you about that,' Raed said, too late.

'I just… I'm sorry.' Soraya didn't know if she'd broken some kind of protocol by stepping out there first without Raed.

'I guess there's more interest in me coming out of the wilderness than I thought too. Rumours will no doubt be circulating already that I'm ready to take up my rightful position at home, and settle down with a new bride.' He sighed.

It was part of the plan, of course, for them to be seen together, but for a moment she'd forgotten where she was and what she was supposed to be doing. As if she and Raed really were here on some kind of date instead of a royal engagement. This was everything she'd worried about and they'd only been a 'couple' for a short while. It was easy to forget he was heir to the throne when he dropped his surly façade to be nice to her. If he would go back to that arrogant, curt prince who'd met her at first, she might be able to hold onto her heart instead of clinging to him now like a lifeline.

'It's okay.' He rested his chin on top of her head but she could hear the smile in his voice. 'But you don't have to do this alone. I know it can all be a bit overwhelming but we're in this together, okay?'

He tilted her chin up so she would look at him and believe he wasn't going to let her face the crowd alone again. Not knowing it wasn't their public relationship that was giving her palpitations.

She swallowed hard. 'Okay.'

'You ready?'

No.

'Yes.'

Raed took her hand. 'Then let's get this over with.'

They walked out onto the balcony and she clung to his arm as though her life depended on it, relying on him to guide her through this charade. A wall of cheers and whoops went up as they announced their relationship to the waiting crowd with a smile and a wave. Once the noise began to subside, and people got used to the idea, they retreated back inside.

'That should give them what they wanted.

Thank you, Soraya, for doing this, and for saving my father's life, if I haven't already said it.'

'You're welcome, although I have to say this is scarier than performing a life-saving operation on a king.'

Raed sighed. 'I know. Zara hated the idea of it too. Not everyone is cut out for this world, myself included, but I guess I don't have a choice any more. I tried the anonymous life but family duty comes first, right?'

She nodded. Like her, Raed had to put his family's needs above his own. Although there would have been greater consequences involved if he hadn't stepped up and worked so hard to provide some stability at a vulnerable time for his family and the country.

'I guess it would have been too much of a culture shock for her.'

He grimaced. 'It wasn't only that. I don't think she loved me enough to give up life in London and venture out here with me when the time came.'

'I'm sorry. It's not nice having someone you love let you down like that.'

His shrug didn't convince Soraya that he was able to dismiss what had happened so easily. 'Perhaps I didn't give her reason enough to want to follow me. It's not easy for me to open up to people. In hindsight maybe she thought I didn't love her enough to make it work.'

Raed's admission made her heart ache for him but also made her feel privileged that he had confided in her about some of his very personal struggles. 'You do have a reputation for being very…closed off.'

Her carefully chosen words earned her a grin and the relief of not having offended him. 'The result of my upbringing, I'm afraid. The royal family aren't supposed to show emotion in public. And when you're schooled in hiding them it becomes very difficult to express yourself in private too. I guess they're the one thing I was able to control when everything else was decided for me—school, where I lived, what I did, what I was going to do. I guess going into medicine was my way of breaking out of that, but we both know that didn't work out when I'm back here. My emotions are the last thing I'm able to have for myself. Often to my detriment. It doesn't mean I don't feel anything, just that I don't like to give away that part of me.'

It was a revealing insight as to why he appeared so cut off at times. Soraya had some experience of not showing her emotions in front of Isolde in order to protect her, and also to prevent herself from losing control. Growing up, with her little sister relying on her, they couldn't have afforded for Soraya to fall apart. She began to wonder if, like Raed, she'd also been guilty of holding back a part of herself from Frank too. Not giving herself completely to him, so she could maintain a little control. It was possible he'd picked up on that and gone searching for that missing part of their marriage in someone else.

'I can relate to that. Though you've been very honest with me about everything that's going on in your life.' She had to wonder why.

'True. And I haven't always been proud of the way I acted in front of you. It's a big deal for me and I'm thankful that you've been very gracious in helping me out.'

Given his reputation and the way he'd sometimes been around her after one of his emotional displays, Soraya knew he'd struggle to come to terms with showing her that part of him. She was grateful, if baffled, that he'd felt able to be honest with her but not someone he'd been in an actual relationship with.

'I don't imagine any of this is easy for you. Especially coming home after such a long time away.'

It occurred to her that Raed would have had to adjust several times over. First in leaving his royal status behind to train as a surgeon in England, and learning to become a mere civilian again. Only to have to adapt again by coming back and giving up that person he'd become. He had responsibilities and duties to carry out, but it would never be the same as the job he'd done here. Swapping the life of a busy surgeon, working in exhilarating, highly dramatic and emotional circumstances, to wave and hand out prizes would be something of an anticlimax. All that hard work training for the specialised role seemed wasted, traded in to be a spectator at a horse show.

He stared at her for what felt like a long time, before answering. 'Sorry. I don't recall anyone asking me how I felt about coming back. My family just expected me to do it and Zara blamed me for ruining our life together by even considering it. No one seemed to care what I was going through, torn between two worlds, having to decide whether to go with my head or my heart. Either way it meant losing someone I cared about, and in the end I had to think about the bigger picture. About what Amir and Farah were going through, and what would happen if Father died. I'd spent years pretending to be someone I wasn't and reality eventually caught up with me that I can't have it all.'

'You wanted a different life. I think most of us have at some point, and there's nothing wrong with that. The fact that you're doing this for your family's sake is honourable and I know things didn't work out with Zara, but at least you tried.'

That burden of responsibility to make the right decision had weighed heavily on her shoulders at times too when she and Isolde had been growing up. She was sure she hadn't always got it right but everything she'd done had been with the best of intentions for her little sister. It was clear Raed had made his choice to give up everything he had here with the welfare of his loved ones uppermost in his mind.

'I tried… Do you think I could use that as a defence when this all comes crumbling down around me again?' His half-smile and the slump in his shoulders gave Soraya an insight into how the real Raed was struggling with the pressure and she wished she could help.

'Hey, you're doing your best. That's all anyone can ask of you.'

'I'm not so sure I did my best for Zara. I don't know if I fought hard enough for our relationship, or thought enough about her feelings. I certainly should have been honest with her about the possibility I'd have to take up my royal duties again instead of dropping her into the midst of the storm.' He raked his hand through his hair, making Soraya itch to comb the few errant strands he'd mussed back into place.

'Perhaps, though it sounds to me like you both could have communicated better. Not that I'm an expert. My husband was cheating on me, spending every penny we had on another woman, and I had no clue. Clearly he wasn't happy in our marriage and I was completely oblivious, believing I was married to a wonderful man who was never home because he was spending all of his time fighting for worthwhile causes. He was a lawyer who worked with charities and organisations for disadvantaged minorities in the community. But he was also a liar, a cheat, and a terrible husband as it turned out.'

'I'm sorry. You deserve better than that.'

She shrugged, having done enough crying and soul-searching over why her marriage had failed. 'Perhaps I was guilty of neglecting Frank's feelings in some ways too, keeping too close an eye on Isolde and how her life was going to pay enough attention to my own.'

'It sounds to me as though you're a great big sister and he should have supported all of you, as a family.'

'Ditto with Zara,' she said, offering him a consolatory smile, astounded that they had dysfunctional families in common. Albeit on opposite sides of the class system.

'You don't have any other family to turn to for help when you need it?'

She shook her head. 'Our parents had us quite late in life and they died within a year of one another from lung cancer when we were young. I did a lot of the parenting, along with caring for Mum and Dad, then became her legal guardian at eighteen. I guess I've never stopped looking out for her.'

'It's understandable.'

'We've both been through a lot. That's why this charity means so much to me. With your financial aid I'm hoping we can get a centre built for young carers, and their families, where they can get the support we never had.'

'I'm sorry you've been dragged into our mess in order to get that funding.'

'Yeah, it's so inconvenient being here in a private box with the most eligible man in the country drinking champagne and waiting for a show in his honour.' If they could keep this level of light-hearted teasing going, instead of counselling each other over the heavy emotional baggage they shared, she might just survive this fake relationship.

There was a light rap on the door and their

waiter came bustling in, followed by a slew of other catering staff all carrying trays.

'If I'd known champagne was all that was needed to keep you happy here, I wouldn't have bothered with this,' he said, directing the staff to leave their assortment of platters and delights.

'What is all this?' She moved closer to the now full table to marvel at the food laid out for them.

Raed set out two small china cups and saucers and began to pour from the silver teapot that had been provided. 'Some good old fish, chips and mushy peas.'

Soraya wanted to protest, tell him it was too much, when the gesture went beyond a mere token to satisfy her hunger. This was a kind attempt to put her at ease, and provide the plain food she had been craving.

'I love a chippy tea, but you really shouldn't have done all this for me.' She took a seat at the table, letting Raed serve her.

'It's my pleasure. My way of thanking you for helping my family and understanding our predicament.' He offered her the plate of buttered white bread that proved he was very much a local.

'I think you're going to have to hire a crane to lift me out of here after I eat all this.'

'Don't worry, you're not going into this alone. I've got your back,' Raed said, with a serious scowl he was clearly struggling to maintain.

Then he smiled that brilliant white smile as he made himself a chip butty, and Soraya realised there was no hope for her poor heart after all.

Raed took a bite from his chip sandwich before he said anything else he'd come to regret. From the moment he had proposed this idea he'd known it was a mistake, yet they hadn't been able to come up with an alternative plan to cover up what was happening with his father. Now Soraya was hopefully going to save the day for them, he'd become protective of her. Perhaps even more so than with Zara.

He'd been so caught up in his own feelings about having to go and be part of the family he'd been born into that he'd failed to recognise Zara's struggles in time and he didn't want to make the same mistake with Soraya. If she was overwhelmed by the crowds and attention, he would do his utmost to make her more comfortable.

The only drawback to that was the look of gratitude she gave him every time he did something nice for her. Those big blue eyes could persuade him to do anything. Not ideal when he was supposed to be keeping his distance. Something that was becoming increasingly hard to do when they appeared to have so much in common. She was the only person in his life to date who seemed to understand his struggle with family responsibility and it was difficult to walk away from someone who listened, who empathised with him, and sacrificed her own happiness for others too.

'Thank you again,' she said, pouring herself another cup of tea.

'You're welcome.'

Soraya took another bite of her butty, leaving her top lip smeared with butter.

'You've got something on your lip.' He pointed towards the butter rather than risk touching her himself and experiencing another one of those shock waves through his body that seemed to happen every time he laid a hand on her.

'Oops.' She attempted to wipe it away with a napkin, completely missing the spot.

'It's still there.' He tried again, only to put himself through agony watching her tongue search around her mouth instead.

'Here, let me,' he said in the end, somewhat abruptly, and leaned in to sweep it away with his thumb.

'Thanks.'

He was aware of the breathy tone in her voice, of her eyes watching him intently as he came closer, and when he licked the butter off his thumb, he saw her pupils dilate. And knew he had to get the hell out of there.

'I think it's starting. We should go and show our faces, put on an act of unity.' Raed scrambled to his feet, knocking the table and spilling his tea in the process.

'I'll clear this up first.' Soraya began to dab at the spilt tea with a napkin but Raed needed out of this enclosed space. It sounded ridiculous even to him but he thought he would breathe better outside with the crowd of thousands, rather than in here with just Soraya sharing the oxygen.

'No. Someone else will do it. We can't miss the opening ceremony.' He would have gone out by himself except that would have defeated the whole purpose of bringing her here in the first place.

After several deep breaths she took his hand and they walked out. The crowd went wild as they waved and bathed in the attention their relationship received. As the national anthem played they remained standing, paying respect to the country. Raed thought of his country and became a little choked up realising how close they had come to losing his father, and how this could all be for him at home some day. It was overwhelming and he was glad when they were finally able to take their seats again.

'Are you okay?' As perceptive as ever, Soraya leaned across to check on him.

'Yes. I think the moment just got to me. I've been so busy trying to cover everything up, holding things together, it's only now I'm realising what might have happened if my father had died. We'd be a country in mourning, in turmoil, with my life in even more disarray than it already is. I don't even know if they would want me to be King, or if that's what I want. At least we've got more time before we have to deal with all of that and we've got you to thank for that.'

He'd treated her as an inconvenience when they'd first met, but Soraya had become an asset to the whole family. The only good thing to happen to him in a year.

'Just doing my job,' she nonchalantly responded to him pouring his heart out. But they both knew she'd done much more than that.

CHAPTER FIVE

ONCE THE INTEREST in them had died down and the event started, Soraya was able to relax and forget about being on show herself with the focus on the horses and riders. The dressage event had Soraya mesmerised. The riders had such control over the horses' every movement she knew it must have taken years of dedication and hard work to gain the animals' trust.

'Do you ride?' she asked Raed, curious if he could wield the same power over these huge beasts as he did with humans.

'I used to. It's expected of the royal family to have some level of ability. Not as much for going into battle any more, but at least for ceremonial purposes. It's been a while for me though. There wasn't much opportunity for me to ride in the city.' With another insight into Raed's life came a sadness in his eyes. One that she recognised, which told of personal sacrifice and a wish for more in life. It seemed wealth and privilege couldn't free an eldest child of responsibilities either.

'Yeah, I can't say it was practical for us in London either. Or financially viable.'

'It must have been tough, raising your sister alone and putting yourself through medical school. I know I rebelled against my family, but I wasn't against taking their money to pay for my schooling.' It was clear he thought himself a hypocrite in doing so, but Soraya knew she would've done the same thing.

'Listen, I've done the scrimping and saving and scrabbling to pay the bills. There's no shame in accepting a helping hand, and no gold medals handed out for struggling alone.' It would have made her life so much easier if she'd had financial support at least trying to raise Isolde and manage her studies at the same time. Then she wouldn't have had to add the stress of a waitressing job on top of it all.

'Maybe we should start giving them out.'

'To be honest, I think any families who are going through what we did would appreciate financial aid rather than a symbolic gesture.' It was too late for her and Isolde, and, even though Raed was probably joking, the memory of that time was still raw for her. When Frank had come into her life, seemingly fighting for disadvantaged families like hers, she'd been blinded by his goodness. She hadn't discovered what lurked behind that altruism until it was too late.

Raed's sudden lapse into silence made her wonder if she'd overstepped the mark by speaking her mind so bluntly. When he was chatting so casually to her it was easy to forget it was royalty she was talking to. Despite the years he'd spent out of the country, he had no real concept what it was like to struggle to pay for basic amenities when, by his own admission, his family had continued to pay all of his bills when he'd left home.

It wasn't his fault any more than her circumstances had been something she'd had any control over, but trying to survive on very little money, counting every penny, left scars. She had a different life now but those memories were the very reason she found it hard to shake off that imposter syndrome. Especially here, pretending to be part of Raed's world, where food could be demanded on a whim and people made horses dance for your entertainment.

'Perhaps it is about time we did something for disadvantaged families. As you say, meaningless gestures might salve our social conscience, but they don't put food on the table.'

'I'm sorry, I didn't mean to be so rude. It's just a touchy subject, that's all.'

'No, you're right. If I'm fated to be in this position I should do something more than complain. I could make a difference and give the royal family some meaning rather than simply being a meaningless symbol. When I'm in charge I could make changes that benefit the people of our country. We could give scholarships to some of the families that wouldn't otherwise be able to afford a university education, or run schemes to help with childcare for single-parent families.'

'That's a great idea, Raed. I'm sure you could make such a difference.'

'You know what, I think it'd give me a real sense of purpose too. There are so many areas of social deprivation that need attention and I think my family have been blind, sitting up there on our jewelled thrones. I have you to thank for opening my eyes. Maybe I'll name the scholarship after you.'

He was so animated about the whole thing, so enthused about making a difference it was difficult to tell if he was serious about that last part. Soraya didn't care as long as it meant there would be help available for families who couldn't see an end in sight to their struggle.

This decision to better himself, to use his position to help others, only made Raed seem more attractive. With every second she spent getting to know him, that tough outer exterior fell away. The cool, efficient surgeon showing the warm, kind man he was at heart. Soraya really should have learned her lesson about falling for men who championed passionately for others.

Unfortunately, it seemed as though she was a lost cause.

CHAPTER SIX

RAED COULD BARELY focus on the rest of the events, even though Soraya was beside him clapping at every horse jump and wincing at those who didn't manage to clear the bars. His mind was buzzing with ideas of how the family could contribute to society beyond being merely decorative. Part of what made his job as a surgeon so rewarding was being able to make a difference to people's lives, and knowing that his life had meaning too. To have that taken away from him had made him question his own worth. Especially when Zara hadn't found sufficient reason to stay with him.

Due to her impoverished and difficult background, Soraya was clearly finding some aspects of his lifestyle challenging too, but with one huge difference. Instead of simply shutting down and rejecting it, she'd been able to make him see how he could turn things to everyone's advantage. She was offering him solutions to his problem, using his position to do good and giving him a reason to carry on. They'd communicated more in the space of a few days than he had in seven years with Zara.

If he was honest though, it was his fault she hadn't been prepared to deal with the idea of his real identity, his duty to his country. In pretending that part of his life wasn't happening, that he would never have to return to it, he'd been lying to himself and Zara.

It would always have fallen to him to return home—it was his birthright, his responsibility. Trying to run away from it had been stupid and naïve, but also damaging to his relationship. It had proved the lack of real trust between them when he'd kept that information from her, and he knew Zara had felt betrayed. Raed couldn't keep blaming her for everything that had gone wrong when he'd played a huge part in the breakdown of the relationship.

It had taken being with Soraya to see how much he had kept hidden from Zara. Not only did Soraya know about all the skeletons in his closet, she had helped to keep the door shut on them.

If he and Zara had talked the way he and Soraya had, been honest about what they wanted, or what they were struggling with, they might have been able to salvage their relationship. The fact that they hadn't even tried suggested it was over long before his father's health issues had forced him to think about going home.

The only problem with that realisation was the thought he should have been with someone like Soraya from the start. There was more than her beauty that drew Raed to her, and they were getting closer by the minute. However, it wasn't going to do him any good to start believing Soraya could be the woman he needed, who would be there for him the way Zara hadn't been, when she'd be out of his life as soon as his father was well on the way to recovery.

'I should probably go down there and meet some of the riders, shake a few hands and hooves.' Near the end of the event he made a move to leave and put some space between him and Soraya. They'd played the role of lovestruck couple and he didn't want to get too carried away with the idea. Some time refocusing as a VIP here would remind him that there were more important issues at stake other than his love life. He was here representing his father, the King, not Raed the lonely surgeon who was apparently still hoping he'd find his soulmate.

'Should I come down with you?' Soraya rose hesitantly from her chair and he was tempted to tell her to stay where she was, but it wouldn't have been fair to leave her here on her own. She didn't know anyone here, or what was expected of her. He'd simply dropped her in the middle of his world and expected her to adapt. A mistake he'd made once before.

'Sure. You can stay in the background if you don't want to get involved but you can come down behind the scenes at least.' He let the security team know of their plans so they could escort them down.

At least when they were being taken through private exits and secret corridors they didn't have to keep up the pretence with physical contact. Holding hands or placing an arm around Soraya's waist might seem innocuous in itself, but, in tandem with his growing emotional connection to her, the slightest touch was becoming so much more. With every interaction and shared secret their connection grew stronger and he couldn't afford to form another attachment with someone who was ultimately going to leave him to deal with everything on his own again here.

'It's true what they say about royalty.' Soraya waited until they were in the elevator before she spoke.

'What's that?'

'That you must think the whole world smells of fresh paint.' She grinned and pointed at the expensive wallpaper that lined the back of the lift, clearly added recently to give it more of a regal feel for his benefit.

He hadn't noticed until she'd pointed it out to him. Something else he'd taken for granted and he thought of all the extra work that had undoubtedly gone on in the background to prepare for his visit. Yet another example of his obliviousness when it came to people around him. It was about time he appreciated his status and the effort others went to in order to make him comfortable. He made a note to give his thanks to the venue staff for their contribution to his visit, as it was the least he could do here. Once he was back at the palace he was going to make enquiries about how to make a greater difference to the people of their country.

The competitors lined up with their horses for the meet and greet and Soraya stood at the perimeter of the jumping ground while Raed went along the line.

'Well done.'

'Great show.'

'Congratulations.'

He smiled, shook hands and took an interest in every one of the people he was introduced to, all the time aware that Soraya was close by and wanting to show her that he wasn't some spoiled rich brat who didn't appreciate his privileged position.

'Thank you for coming, Your Royal Highness.' The organiser stepped forward and introduced himself as Ranj Abdallah.

'My pleasure. You put on an excellent show and I'm sure it's done a lot for the tourist industry here.' The international competitors would be a boost to the local economy by staying in local hotels and availing themselves of the hospitality services nearby. It was something they should capitalise on in the future and work to make bigger and better to attract more foreign interest.

'Well, thank you, sir. It's nice to be appreciated.' Ranj's smile and the proud puffing out of his chest told Raed praise wasn't something often dished out by his father at such occasions. He thought it was about time that changed. If the royal family wanted more respect they had to earn it by showing that they appreciated people and becoming more of an asset to those around them at home, rather than simply living off their taxes.

'I'd like to talk to you some time about perhaps setting up a charity event to raise funds for disadvantaged members of our society. In return you can count on my patronage and whatever influential connections I can bring to the table.'

'I—I'd like that very much, sir.' Forgetting himself for a moment, and royal protocol, Ranj shook Raed's hand enthusiastically.

It wasn't a fully-fledged plan but at least by voicing his intentions out loud he was committing to the new project. The details could be fleshed out later, hopefully with his parents' approval and co-operation too.

'Great. We'll get something in the diary.' Raed handed him his business card. He knew he was taking a risk arranging this without running it past the official channels first, but he was keen to start making decisions, and a difference, as soon as possible. Along with telling Soraya the news of his plans. He wanted to impress her, show her that he could use his position to help others, and there was also a futile hope that she could somehow be a part of it all. Nonsense, of course, when she had a life in England, but in an ideal world he'd have someone like Soraya supporting him and working with him instead of only seeing the negatives in this way of life.

Just as he turned to walk back towards Soraya there was a loud bang, which echoed around the arena, causing screams and panic and his security team to rush at him. Raed's first thought was for Soraya, who looked scared to death. His personal bodyguard was trying to bundle him out of the arena altogether, but he wouldn't leave her. If this was some sort of terrorist attack or attempted assassination, she was as much of a target as he was, if not more when he'd left her unprotected.

All hell had broken loose around them with people rushing towards the exits and onto the showground. Horses that had been spooked by the bang were running amok around the arena, some trailing their trainers, others blinded by panic taking the jumps on their own. Raed's instinct was to wrap his arms around Soraya to protect her body with his and in that moment he came to realise how important she'd become to him, given he was willing to put his own life on the line for hers.

He brushed away the usual protocol to get him out of harm's way as soon as possible, concerned only with Soraya's well-being. 'Are you okay?'

'Yeah, just a little shaken.' There was a tremor in her voice, her eyes wide with fear, but no visible signs that she'd been hurt.

The relief that washed over Raed was akin to that he'd experienced after his father's heart bypass when he knew he was out of immediate danger. But Soraya wasn't family and it was strange that he should feel so strongly about keeping her safe. Of course, as a medic he always did his best to save people, but his urge to protect Soraya in that moment was something more, came from somewhere deeper than a sense of duty and compassion for another human being. It spoke volumes about the bond they'd forged over such a short time, but was also going to make saying goodbye harder than he'd ever imagined when the time came.

'We really need to get you out of here, sir.' Now he knew Soraya was safe he was willing for them both to be transferred somewhere by the security team.

The Tannoy crackled to life. 'Ladies and gentlemen, please do not panic. We have confirmation that the blast you heard was caused by an electrical surge. There is no threat to life but we need to evacuate the building. Please make your way quickly and calmly to the exit.'

Raed turned to look back at the scenes unfolding in the wake of the unexpected incident. Now he knew there was no immediate threat, that they weren't under attack, the urgency to run lessened, even though he still wanted to get Soraya away from any potential danger.

'Take Ms Yarrow back to the palace. I want to make sure everyone here is okay first.'

His decision to see if he could be of any assistance was met with protests all around.

'I don't think that's a good idea, sir.'

'I'm not leaving without you. I can help too.' Soraya brushed off any suggestion that she should be taken to safety and leave him to deal with matters here alone.

He briefly considered using his influence to insist the team take her out of harm's way but, apart from the determined look in her eyes and the stubborn folded-arms stance, he wanted her to stay with him. She was capable and courageous, and exactly who he needed to help him with this crisis.

'In that case it looks as though we're all here for the foreseeable future.' Raed ventured back out onto the arena floor to see the aftermath with the entourage in tow.

The trainers and riders were trying to rein in the horses, the spectators had thinned out and were now moving towards the exits in a calmer manner, assisted by stewards and security. However, there were a few casualties on the ground being attended to, including Ranj, the event organiser, who was stretched out and seemingly unconscious.

Raed bent down to speak to the first aider by his side who was tending to a nasty wound on the man's head.

'What happened?'

'One of the horses got spooked, kicked out and struck Ranj on the head. He's breathing but hasn't responded to me. I've phoned for an ambulance but I'm worried about his head injury.'

'I'm a doctor, let me take a look.' Raed pulled off his jacket to cover Ranj's body and keep him warm, and rolled up his own shirt sleeves. All thoughts of his ceremonial role were forgotten as his medical instincts kicked in.

'Why don't you go and tend to some of the others needing help? We're both doctors, we can handle him until the paramedics arrive.' Soraya rested a hand gently on the man's shoulder, relieving him of his responsibility here. Although there were people at these events trained in first aid, Ranj had two experienced surgeons more than capable of taking care of his injuries.

'If you're sure.' The man looked towards Raed for confirmation it was okay to leave his post.

'Soraya's a doctor too. Thanks for your help but we can take it from here.' It was important to him that her capabilities be recognised too. That she wasn't just here as his fiancée, or someone to hand-hold the injured, and they were lucky to have someone with her skills in attendance. While 'doctor' couldn't adequately describe her talents in the medical field, it did justify her place here in as few words as necessary.

It was sufficient explanation for the man to leave them.

'But leave us some of your first-aid supplies before you go, please,' Soraya added, taking possession of some dressings and bandages.

Ranj had been moved into the recovery position and, though he was breathing, a serious injury like a kick to the head meant his condition could change at any time.

'Ranj, can you hear me? It's Raed. You've had a blow to the head. The ambulance will be here soon but I need you to squeeze my hand if you can hear me.' There was no response.

Soraya knelt down and began to dab the wound at his temple, cleaning the area so they could see how bad the injury was beneath all the blood. 'Raed, there's clear fluid leaking from his ears and nose.'

It was bad news. Raed knew that this was a sign that Ranj's head trauma had caused a leak of cerebrospinal fluid from around the brain. An indicator that there might be a fracture of the skull, or a subdural haematoma where blood had collected causing pressure inside the skull. If left untreated it could lead to meningitis or seizures, but, with Ranj remaining unresponsive, they had no way to gauge his symptoms.

'We need to get him to hospital for MRI and CT scans to see exactly what is going on in there. The sooner he gets treatment, the quicker he will recover.' Raed was tempted to get him into the back of the limo and take him to the hospital himself until he heard the sirens and knew help was on the way.

'Medic! We need a medic over here,' someone shouted from across the arena.

When they looked over to the source it was to see a man cradling a woman in his lap, clearly distressed and in desperate need of attention.

'You go, Soraya. I'll stay here with Ranj.' He didn't think twice about enlisting her help and she certainly didn't need him to supervise when she'd just successfully operated on a king.

Soraya grabbed some medical supplies, kicked off her shoes, hitched up her dress, and sprinted barefoot over to the couple. She wasn't someone afraid to get her hands, or feet, dirty, and always put others before herself. A flaw they both suffered from.

'Ranj, if you can hear me, please open your eyes.' There was no response. 'An ambulance is on the way. Hopefully it will be here soon.'

While Raed tried again to rouse his patient he could see Soraya setting to work on the woman across the way. She appeared to be making a tourniquet around the woman's leg, and commandeering people's jackets to cover the woman's body, probably in an attempt to keep her warm and prevent shock from setting in. When she began dismantling the horse jumps and using them to prop the leg, stabilising it so as not to exacerbate the injury, he figured it was a fracture she was dealing with. Likely caused in the crush.

Raed smiled at her ingenuity. Soraya wasn't prone to panic and simply got on with the task at hand, something that stood her in good stead in her career, but also a quality he admired in her in general. He'd asked a lot of her lately, and though she hadn't always been happy to oblige, she'd done so to the best of her abilities. At times he felt as though she was the only one he had on his side helping him navigate the new direction his life had taken and he was grateful to have her.

They both sat with their respective patients until the ambulances arrived to transport the casualties to hospital. As the most serious of the casualties, Ranj was lifted into the ambulance first.

'I'll come with him. I'm a neurosurgeon. I might be needed to assist at the hospital.'

'Your Royal Highness, we can't possibly let

you travel alone in the ambulance,' his body-guard reminded him, putting him firmly back into his princely role.

'Then we can follow in the limo.' Undeterred, Raed insisted that they continue to the hospital, though he drew the line at the whole team waiting with him for news.

'Soraya? Would you like to come with us?' He caught up with her as she loaded her patient onto the ambulance. This time he knew better than to try and send her back to the palace when he knew her work ethic was just as strong as his.

'Yes. I think it's a clean break but I'd like to make sure. How's Ranj?'

'The same. Unresponsive. That's why I'd like to go and see if I can be of any assistance.'

Once the ambulances were safely loaded and on their way to the hospital, sirens blaring, Raed and Soraya got into the limo.

'Thank you for your help back there.' Sitting close on the back seat of the car, he could see her dress was torn and dirty now, her make-up all but gone, and her hair in disarray around her shoulders. She'd never looked so beautiful.

'It's my job. My real job, not the pretend one.' Soraya smiled as she teased.

'You've certainly made an impression today.' Raed was sure if there had been any opposition to his new romantic interest, her skills and compassion today would have won everyone over, just as they had him.

'Can I go home, then?' She laughed, but, even in jest, the words struck Raed hard.

He wasn't ready for her to leave him. It was the first time he'd really felt as though he had support, emotionally and physically. Soraya had been there for him when he'd been going through a difficult personal time, and now she was here assisting him in a medical capacity too. It was the crossover between his two worlds that he'd thought he'd never achieve with anyone else. And now he'd found a certain acceptance of his royal role again, aided by Soraya, he wasn't sure he'd ever be ready for her to leave.

Soraya was exhausted, and she was sure Raed was drained. It was a lot to cope with between his father's health, coming back home as part of a lie, and then getting caught up in an emergency medical incident. In a way she was glad she'd come to Zaki with him so he didn't have to deal with everything on his own. She knew how that isolation felt, having to shoulder all the responsibility of the family.

Today had also given her an insight into his professional manner. He had a reputation as being stern and efficient but she could see that was simply because he was so focused on his job. She would even forgive him for telling her what to do earlier because she understood his need to take charge in that scenario. A medical situation was one thing he could control, unlike the rest of his life.

Soraya felt bad for him that he'd been put in this position. She'd be able to walk away from it eventually but he never could, as events had proven. Despite his efforts to hide it, she knew there was a vulnerable side to him that struggled with his burden. She'd seen it, recognised herself in it, along with that feeling of loneliness. Although she had Isolde and her career back in England, it wasn't going to be easy to leave him here dealing with everything on his own when the time came.

Not least because of the way he'd looked after her today. The gesture of ordering familiar cuisine for her so she didn't feel so out of place had been sweet, and she would have put it down to a simple act of hospitality if it weren't for his behaviour during the scare at the arena. Soraya didn't think his concern for her had merely been a polite display of chivalry.

The way he'd dived upon her, covering her, had been a natural instinct to protect her. A real concern for her welfare when he'd put his own at risk, going against the advice of his security team to save her, and the injured they'd later discovered.

It spoke of a bond between them that came from more than circumstances. There were some emotions involved. And they weren't all hers. They were growing closer all the time, and though she knew it was impossible for them to be together, there was a part of her still leaning towards the notion. As well as being handsome and successful, Raed was loyal and compassionate. Qualities that had sadly been lacking in her husband. She knew expecting anything to happen between them was heartache in waiting when they came from two different worlds, both bound by responsibility. Yet Soraya found herself spinning wildly into the abyss.

Once Soraya had been assured her patient hadn't suffered anything more than a broken leg at the hospital, she came to join Raed waiting for news on Ranj. With no one brave enough to tell him he wasn't needed, he and Soraya were ushered into a private family room with his bodyguard on sentry outside the door.

'I hope he's going to be okay,' Soraya said, worrying her bottom lip with her teeth.

'Me too. We were talking about setting up

a charity event to raise money for our poorer members of society.'

'That sounds really positive, Raed. I'm sure you'll come up with an amazing plan once Ranj has recovered.'

There was something about Soraya's genuine interest, her praise for him, that made him crave more. Talking to her today had really fired him up to generally *be* more. Although the day's events had been shocking and unsettling for all involved, that drama and adrenaline rush of getting involved took him back to his time working in the hospital environment and he knew he wasn't done with that part of his life just yet either.

With the permission of Ranj's family, who were ensconced in another room waiting for news, and Raed's request to be updated about his condition, the A & E consultant came back to see them with the results of the scans and blood tests they'd run on his patient's admission to the emergency department.

'Mr Abdallah's apparent head trauma this afternoon has indeed caused a subdural haematoma, as you'd suspected, Your Royal Highness.'

'Please, just call me Raed.' He knew no one here would but this occasion wasn't about him or his family. Here he was simply asking to be treated as another medical colleague with a professional and personal interest in the patient.

'Mr Abdallah is going to require surgery to relieve the pressure on his brain. He still hasn't gained consciousness so we are hoping to get the surgeon here as soon as possible.'

'You don't have someone available now?'

The consultant went red in the face. 'I'm afraid not. We don't have the budget to keep a specialist permanently on call here. It will be a while before the one in the city hospital can get here.'

It appeared their health service was one more area that had been neglected lately and he knew it was because the family had been too distracted by their own personal problems to focus on any fundraisers or personal appearances, which could have helped to boost the hospital coffers. They had their own private team of highly skilled professionals to call on when they were sick and it didn't seem fair to expect those born into less wealthy families not to have access to the same levels of care.

'I'll do it.'

'But, sir—'

'Raed, are you sure?'

He understood the consultant and Soraya's concerns but this wasn't simply a knee-jerk reaction because he was invested in this patient now. 'I'm a highly qualified, respected brain surgeon. I've performed this procedure hundreds of times. You can wait until your own surgeon arrives but I'm here and time is of the essence. The longer we wait to relieve that pressure on Ranj's brain, the more we risk serious long-term effects.'

'I'll talk to the family.' The consultant left and Raed knew he'd be scrubbing in again for perhaps the last time.

'Raed, are you sure about this?' Soraya asked, her brow creased with concern he knew was for him just as much as it was for Ranj.

'I've never been more sure about anything in my life. Life-saving brain surgery I can do. I'm infinitely more comfortable in an operating theatre than a royal box, and certainly more useful.' That seemed enough to convince Soraya that he knew what he was doing, although guaranteed success would be the only way his father would ever have agreed to such extreme measures. Something a surgeon could never truly offer when surgery always came with risks of complication, but Raed was confident enough in his abilities and himself to undertake the procedure, anticipating a positive outcome.

'In that case, could I assist you? Two surgeons are better than one, right? I mean, you'd obviously take the lead on this but I would like to help.'

Sometimes having two surgeons working alongside one another caused a clash of egos, but Raed knew that wouldn't happen with Soraya because, just like today, his overwhelming want to be with her overruled his head.

CHAPTER SEVEN

Raed never ceased to amaze her. Not only was he preparing to give up the life he'd built for himself in England to aid his family, but he was also still working to help everyone who crossed his path. He seemed really excited about the charity event he'd been talking to Ranj about hosting and Soraya had a feeling it would be the first of many fund-raising projects he'd undertake now he was getting used to his position back in the family again. If only she'd had someone like Raed to help her and Isolde growing up they might not have struggled so much. She was proud of him and the work he was doing. Including now, performing this craniotomy on Ranj.

'Scalpel,' Raed demanded before making an incision into Ranj's scalp to make a window flap of skin where he could access the skull easily.

Although Soraya was every bit as capable a

surgeon as Raed, she had her own area of expertise and respected that he was the expert in this field. On this occasion, she was content to merely assist.

'Drill, please.' He cut away a section of the skull to reveal the bleed beneath.

'I need someone to suction and irrigate.'

'I've got it.' Soraya was glad to have something to do, though the other theatre staff were probably capable of doing the task without her.

She suctioned away the blood so Raed could see where he was working and cleaned the area with water. It was clear why he had such a stellar, if not warm, reputation. He was completely focused on the task at hand, as a good surgeon should be. Okay, so he didn't hold full conversations or like to listen to music as he worked like some other surgeons, but that just proved how invested he was in his patient.

Surgery was nothing new to Soraya but she still marvelled as he removed the subdural haematoma, relieving the pressure on the brain. It seemed second nature to him as he replaced the piece of bone and sewed the skin back over the site. Saving someone's life had been commonplace for him once upon a time, and it was a shame for Raed and those who needed his sort of skills that he would no longer be allowed to work in this field.

She could only imagine the uproar at the palace once they found out about this little venture so soon after his public reappearance as the Crown Prince. Still, it might take the heat off her if the focus moved from his new girlfriend to his inability to leave all of his old life behind for good. The strain of faking a relationship for the cameras, all the while yearning for it to be real, was taking a serious toll on her mental health.

Today had shown her how much Raed changed when he was around her. Here in the operating theatre he was precise, exact, almost emotionless. Yet she'd seen quite a different side to him, one that he'd admitted he tried to keep to himself. While she appreciated his cool, calm demeanour was what was needed in surgery, she could understand why it would have caused problems in his personal life. She considered herself fortunate to have seen the real Raed, who'd come to her for help, who got excited about future projects and whose smile made her go weak at the knees. It also made her worry about what they were letting themselves in for by getting so close.

'That was something different,' she commented as they exited the hospital.

'Perhaps it'll make you think about expanding your surgical repertoire,' Raed teased.

'No, thanks, I have plenty of work to keep me busy in cardiology.'

'I'm going to miss it,' he said with a sigh. 'I think that operation was as much for my benefit as Mr Abdallah's. One last hurrah.'

'It would be a shame if you have to give up a job you love when you could help so many families, just because of your position in society.' It was obvious how much he enjoyed his work as a surgeon. She hoped, given some of the changes he was already bringing into effect, he might also be able to find some way of continuing his work at the hospital.

'If there was some way to continue working as well as carrying out my royal duties, I would happily do both. Perhaps you could even join me. I'm sure your skills would be greatly appreciated in the hospital too.'

Even though said in jest, the idea was tempting. Though it wasn't the luxury, or the thought of a new start, that proved the greatest draw. Spending more time with Raed seemed to be something she couldn't resist, despite the issues that would surely bring into her life.

'I'm not sure that's an option,' she said, willing him not to push it any further.

Every second she spent getting to know this man pushed her deeper and dangerously closer to him. Although she didn't want to admit it to herself she liked him, and more than in a professional or friendly capacity. What she was beginning to feel towards him was bringing emotions to the fore that terrified her. He was attractive, yes, rich and powerful, but that paled in significance in the face of his utter kindness. It had always been her weakness, and her undoing.

She'd fallen for that generous spirit once before and it had left her broken-hearted and homeless. Although Raed wasn't likely to leave her paying off his debt, there was a chance she'd find herself a low priority in his life too. Even if he did reciprocate her growing feelings, it was clear today how much other stuff he had going on in his life. All of which he would have to put before a woman. Especially when he'd already lost a relationship because of his dedication to his family and royal duties.

Why should she think she was any different? She wasn't special and certainly not worth him giving up his position in the royal family so she would be number one in his life, nor would she ever ask him to even if he did show any romantic interest in her. However, that was the level of commitment she would need from a man if she was ever to entertain another relationship in the future.

Even if she took the idea of getting involved

with Raed off the cards, she doubted her attraction to him would simply cease because it was inconvenient. If anything, she feared watching him every day proving what a great man he was would make her fall for him harder. It seemed she was doomed to get hurt no matter where she was, but at least if she was in a different country she wouldn't have to see him every day.

'That's a shame. I'm getting used to having you around.' It wasn't the declaration of undying love it would take for her to take a chance on a new relationship, but as he paused to look at her she could see in his eyes he meant every word. But that was what was causing the trouble, wasn't it? She was getting too comfortable with the arrangement too and it wouldn't be long before she believed their fake relationship was real.

'Thanks for your help in theatre today,' Raed said as they made their way back to the car. It had been a long, difficult day for them both and he wasn't sure he would have got through it without Soraya.

'I'm not sure I did anything a theatre nurse couldn't have done.'

'I disagree. My offer still stands. We could use you out here.' Although the initial invitation

to stay had been a spur-of-the-moment suggestion, he didn't regret it. They needed someone
with her expertise in the hospital. In another
time or place he might've decided to set up his
own consultancy, with Soraya on board for all
matters of the heart. It was ironic that was what
was fuelling these incentives to get her to stay
with him too. His heart was making decisions
his head knew would hurt them both.

By her own admission Soraya was scarred
by the end of her relationship, as he was, and
he couldn't offer her any more of himself than
he was able to give to Zara. Same problem, different woman. Soraya needed someone to put
her feelings first, to treat her like the queen
she was, but it couldn't be him when he already had an entire royal family to think about,
not to mention a country. That didn't stop him
wanting her around though. She was a steadying influence on him, a support he desperately
needed.

'You were a big part of the process in getting
me in that theatre again, doing the job I love.' It
was Soraya passionately extolling the need for
something more than awards for poorer families that had got him thinking about the things
he could do rather than those he couldn't. That
new-found belief in his abilities had re-emerged
when Ranj had been hurt. In the future he

might not be able to perform surgery every day the way he used to, but he had been able to do it today. The bonus was having Soraya there with him through it all.

'I don't think you needed much persuading.' She grinned.

'No, but apparently you do.' He stopped walking, afraid once they reached the car and got back to real life they wouldn't have a chance to talk like this again.

'Raed, please don't do this.' She seemed to anticipate what he was going to say, as though she'd been dreading the moment since he'd first suggested staying with him.

'I need you, Soraya.' He wasn't usually one to resort to emotional blackmail but he was a desperate man in need of an ally.

'The longer I'm in your life, the more we'll have to keep up this pretence between us. I don't like lying to people and I don't think I can do it much longer.'

Before Raed could attempt to placate her he heard a rustle in the nearby bushes and spotted a camera lens glinting in the undergrowth. If the press were here there was no way of knowing how much they'd heard, or what would be printed in tomorrow's papers. Even though his father was through his surgery, he was a long way off full recovery and the country was in

Raed's hands until then. The last thing he could afford now was a scandal to break about his fake romance and how it had been a cover for the instability of the current monarchy. He had to act quickly and do something to negate what they already might have overheard.

'In that case, we'll announce the engagement as soon as possible. I know you want time to let your family know what's happening, but I think the truth is going to come out sooner or later.'

He watched Soraya's face contort into a puzzled frown as none of that would have made any sense to her whatsoever.

'What on earth—?'

The second she made it obvious she had no idea what he was talking about the game was over. He would never recover if he was exposed as a liar in the press even if it had been done with the best of intentions. There was only one way he could think of temporarily stopping her from breaking their cover, and, though it might earn him a slap, he had to take the chance. It would be easier to explain things to her later than to the entire country.

Raed grabbed her face in his hands and kissed her hard. He expected the resistance, her attempt to push him away. What he hadn't been prepared for was the way she began to lean into him, her body pressed against his, her mouth softening and accepting his kiss. All notions of the press and what had or hadn't been captured seemed to float out of his brain, replaced only with thoughts about Soraya and how good it felt to have his lips on hers.

She tasted exactly how he'd imagined, sweet and spicy, and infinitely moreish. He couldn't get enough. Soraya's hands, which had been a barrier between their bodies at first, were now wrapped around his neck, her soft breasts cushioned against his chest in the embrace. Every part of him wanted more of her and if they'd been anywhere but in the middle of a car park he might have been tempted to act on that need. It had been a long time since he'd felt this fire in his veins, this passion capable of obliterating all common sense.

He knew this had gone beyond a distraction for any nearby journalists but he didn't want to stop kissing her, touching her, tasting her. Once this stopped and reality came rushing in, he knew he'd never get to do this again.

'Ahem.'

Soraya vaguely acknowledged someone clearing their throat nearby, too deep into the moment to pay it much attention. Raed was kissing her. She didn't know why or what on earth he'd been talking about before launching himself at her, but she could overanalyse that later. Once the kissing was done.

There was another exaggerated cough. 'Your Royal Highness, I really think we should move somewhere more private.'

The warning from Raed's personal protection officer was enough to end the fantasy. There was no way of avoiding the real world with a burly security guard pointing out how indiscreet they were being.

The moment they broke off the kiss, leaving Soraya's head spinning and her lips swollen, she realised there was more behind it than his desperate urge to snog her senseless. Raed was looking around as though watching for someone, waiting for them to be discovered, and his security were trying to bundle them both into the car out of the way.

'What was all that about?'

'I'm so sorry. I spotted a paparazzo hiding in the bushes and panicked. He was bound to have heard our conversation and I just did the first thing that came into my head.'

Through the fog of her kiss-addled brain she recalled a mention of their engagement. 'You knew they were there the whole time?'

He had the decency to look ashamed of himself. 'I needed to give them something more newsworthy. I know it's not the way we had planned for this to come out, but it's more of a story if they think they've discovered it first. If they think we've been hiding the true nature of our relationship from the public. A secret engagement might just about save our backsides.'

'Your backside. It's not going to do much to uncomplicate my life,' she grumbled, trying not to think about his backside and wondering if she'd grabbed hold of it in the heat of the moment. Her cheeks flushed hot enough to rival the passion of that kiss as she thought about the display they'd just put on in front of witnesses, and wondered if it had been captured on camera, ready for the rest of the world to see too.

'I know and I am sorry, but I can't risk this all being revealed as a charade. I'd lose all respect to be caught out in the lies and it wouldn't look favourable for us as a family if the press realised it was all a ruse to cover up news of Father's health.' Although Raed seemed ruffled by the exchange, Soraya was sure it was more to do with what was going to be in tomorrow's headlines than the kiss itself. While she'd been left shaken and stirred by the whole incident.

It was everything she'd been trying to avoid, and apparently with good reason. She resisted the urge to trace her fingers over her lips where Raed had so thoroughly ravished her, still tingling from his touch. Despite the knowledge it had been nothing but another part of the couple disguise, her body was craving more. Raed had awakened that pulsing need for him she'd been trying to bury deep since that first time she'd touched him. Now she knew the rest of his body could match the promise she'd seen sometimes when he looked at her, as though he was ready to devour her, one kiss was never going to be enough. Yet she knew it was all they'd have when she was nothing more than a convenient explanation for his version of the truth.

'And how are we supposed to proceed now? I assume a royal engagement isn't going to stay as a rumour only, if you want to keep your father buried under the headlines until he's ready to take back his throne.' Soraya tried to get them back on track but she was mad at herself for getting swept up in it all. Her reaction to the kiss had been real, those feelings she'd desperately been holding back suddenly surging forward because in that moment she'd believed they were reciprocated.

To find out it had all been a ploy to throw reporters off the scent of the real story going on behind the scenes was crushing. He had been acting a part while she had thrown caution into gale-force winds and kissed him with abandon. Now there was no going back and she couldn't simply stuff those emotions back inside. She didn't know how she was going to survive the rest of her time here harbouring feelings for him she knew were hopeless. Apart from the fact he obviously saw her only as a decoy for press attention, they were a complete mismatch.

Soraya needed a man who would put her first, and he deserved a partner who would support him unconditionally. They both had too many responsibilities to make those sorts of promises to one another. Even if he ever wanted her for more than an extra pair of hands at the hospital.

She cringed, imagining what had been going through Raed's head as she'd wrapped her body around his, totally invested in them as a couple in that moment. Still, she supposed they'd put on a good show and that had been Raed's aim. Mission accomplished.

Raed grimaced, as though he'd just remembered her throwing herself at him too. 'We are going to have to make the announcement.'

'Okay. I guess that's why I'm here. That's what I agreed to.' She had to remind herself of that. It wasn't Raed's fault he didn't have feelings for her, or that she'd mistaken their arrangement for something more. But it didn't make it any easier to feign enthusiasm for the prospect of their fake engagement.

Something Raed seemed to pick up on. 'You know the position I'm in, Soraya. I'm sorry. I didn't want any of this.'

His words didn't make the current situation any less painful or humiliating. At least the kissing part. The fraudulent relationship, being press fodder, falling for a totally unsuitable prince and throwing herself at him, she could do without.

She watched a lone drop of condensation slip slowly on its sad journey to nowhere down the car window. It was only when it dripped onto her hand that Soraya realised she was watching her own reflection.

Raed's heart should have been full, his morning full of sunshine and rainbows. A check at the hospital had brought the good news that Ranj had had a good night. He had come round some time after the operation, and though surprised by the events relayed to him about how he'd come to be in the hospital, was recovering well.

The first person he'd wanted to share the news with was also the reason he was so blue today, despite everything going to plan so far. Every headline in the morning's papers had been screaming about his romance with Soraya and a write-up about their part in the drama at the horse show, with one paper in particular claiming an exclusive with news of their engagement featured with photographic evidence of their very steamy kiss in the car park. They'd done a good job of convincing their audience that they were a genuine couple judging by the article proclaiming the greatest, most surprising love story of the year. Perhaps too good a job when he'd managed to convince himself it was real too.

The kiss, which should have been a brief interaction solely to give the papers something to talk about, had turned into something much more at his insistence. As soon as his lips had met Soraya's all pretence had vanished, replaced with his very real desire for her. Satisfying his need had come at too high a price now he knew what it was to kiss her, taste her, and want more. Something that could never happen when she was here as a favour, pretending to be his love interest only.

It was unlike him to get carried away the way he had, kissing her so thoroughly, and passionately. But in that moment he'd forgotten all about the donation he'd promised in order to get here, and the whole 'protecting the monarchy' ruse they were engaged in. Selfishly only thinking about what he wanted. Soraya.

When he'd stopped kissing her long enough to think properly, and remembered the reason he'd kissed her in the first place, he could tell it had changed things between them. Soraya was obviously regretting agreeing to this debacle. Even if she had kissed him back, he'd heard it in her voice that she didn't want to go through with the engagement announcement. Despite everything he had on the line, he didn't want to force her into doing something she didn't want to.

Soraya was someone who deserved the world. She'd sacrificed so much in the past to benefit her loved ones it was unfair that people took advantage of her kind nature. Him included. She'd told him she didn't want this fake romance, yet he'd ridden over her wishes at the time because it didn't fit his agenda.

He knocked on her bedroom door. 'Soraya? It's me, Raed. Can we talk?'

He was sure he could hear her moving around in there and the knowledge that she might be avoiding him was a dagger to the heart.

'I don't want to be someone else who takes you for granted and disregards your feelings. If you want to end this now I'll understand. I won't stop you.'

The decision wasn't one he had made easily, because he didn't want to lose her, but that was partly what had caused the problems. He'd put his needs before hers. For now the most important thing for him was to do the right thing, even if that meant letting her go.

Shoulders slumped, he wondered if she'd ever talk to him again as he walked away. She might decide it was easier to jump on a plane and go back to England without another word.

Then the sound of a key turning in a lock echoed along the corridor, followed by the soft pad of footsteps.

By the time Raed had turned around Soraya had already disappeared back into the room, leaving only a scent of roses and a swish of a silk robe in her wake. He followed her like a faithful hound, grateful that she would even give him an audience. Only time would tell if she was simply granting him a last request, or a last-minute reprieve. He crossed his fingers and hoped there was a chance he was enough to make her want to continue.

Soraya was aware she was still in her night-clothes and belted her dressing gown tight around the lacy camisole and knickers she wore. It wasn't an appropriate outfit for dealing with Raed. She didn't need to be at any more of a disadvantage while he was sitting in her bedroom in his power suit. On the same bed she'd lain on all night staring at the ceiling trying to decide what she wanted to do. Now here he was offering her an out, but the very gesture was making her think twice about getting the hell out of here.

'Do you want to end this?' Raed asked again, giving her the choice and complicating everything.

Putting her feelings before her needs was more than anyone else had ever done for her and only made it harder for her to leave. However, her insecurity made her question this sudden turnaround and she wondered if it was because he'd decided she was more trouble than a whole country finding out he'd lied about being in a relationship to hide his father's ill health. If he'd been able to tell she'd put her heart and soul into that kiss and wanted an easy out before he had to let her down gently that he wasn't interested in her.

'No. I said I would go along with it and I will.' She took a seat at the dressing table rather than get cosy next to him on the bed so she could try and keep a clear head. Even the mention of that kiss set her on fire and it wasn't helping seeing him sprawled all over her bed as though he was waiting for her to join him. Apparently it didn't matter to her body that she'd humiliated herself, as she was aching for a repeat performance.

'I've asked and expected too much from you.

You did the job I asked you to do and it's not fair to keep expecting more. I never meant to take advantage of your good nature.'

'Why did you kiss me?' The words burst out of her mouth before her filter could catch it. 'You could have shut me down some other way.'

One of the things keeping her awake last night had been the replay of that kiss over and over again and the knowledge that he could have achieved the same outcome with the press without even touching her.

Raed turned over onto his back, hands behind his head as he stared at the same ceiling she now knew intimately. 'I did what came naturally. I acted on my instinct and that was to kiss you.'

A shiver danced along her spine at the thought he might actually have wanted to kiss her, the same way she'd been yearning for it too.

'If I overstepped the mark, I'm sorry.'

He must have mistaken her silence as a sign she was still in need of an apology. The truth was she didn't need it or want it. What she needed was for Raed to have been invested in that kiss as much as she'd been. Although that would have brought a whole set of new problems for her to deal with.

Ending this was the sensible option, removing herself from temptation and the whole tangled mess of lies she'd found herself wrapped up in. Raed was unattainable, and when this whole fake relationship had run its course she would be surplus to requirements. This was exactly what she needed to get out of here guilt free. So why was her heart insisting that she needed to stay and see what came next after a kiss?

'You did what you had to. But tell me, what's the next step in this great plan?' She didn't want to be taken by surprise again.

'I haven't figured all the details out yet, but we can't put off making the official engagement announcement for ever. I'll go make some calls and let you get dressed.'

Soraya stood to see him to the door, her robe falling open to expose her bare legs, and Raed's gaze lingered there long enough to send her temperature rocketing again.

When he was looking at her like that it made her consider joining him on the bed and finally doing what she wanted for once, to hell with the consequences.

Then Raed bounced back up onto his feet and headed straight for the door, leaving her wondering once again if she'd imagined his interest.

'See you later.' And just like that, he rushed

out of the room, away from whatever was clearly still simmering between them.

The door slammed shut before she could catch up with him and ask what was wrong. Of course, she knew the answer to that because it was the same reason she'd been freaked out last night too. There was an attraction between them, even more dangerous, a connection, that seemed to keep drawing them back to one another, despite the obvious pitfalls.

Soraya threw herself onto the bed, warm from Raed's body, his cologne still hanging in the air. She grabbed the nearest cushion and screamed her frustration into it.

The choice to leave had never really been hers, but at least Raed had let her pretend for a while.

CHAPTER EIGHT

RAED DIDN'T KNOW what had convinced Soraya to continue with the plan any more than what had prompted him to give her an out. Perhaps he'd realised it would be safer for him if she had called it off. Then he wouldn't have to worry about her abandoning him once he was head over heels in love with her because she'd already be gone, crisis averted. Because he knew he was falling for Soraya deeper every day.

It was going to be tough enough to keep seeing her, that attraction seemingly building every day, and he was beginning to believe that she might feel it too after the way she'd returned his kiss. There were so many obstacles in the way of them being a couple, it would be impossible for them to act on that chemistry between them.

Even when he wasn't with her, he was thinking about her and had spent most of the day working on a surprise for her tonight. He knew it was blurring that line between keeping their cover story alive in the press and a personal need to be with her, but he hoped he could persuade her to go along with his plans.

All he'd told her was that she should dress up for dinner. Now he was standing here in a tux, praying she wouldn't stand him up.

Raed looked at his watch, waiting for the hands to reach the time he'd suggested they meet. Sweat began to break out on his forehead as it came and went. If she'd had second thoughts about continuing with this pretend romance he'd be back at square one trying to hold the whole country together on his own until his father had recovered.

'Sorry I'm late. I couldn't decide what to wear. Especially when I don't know where we're going.' Soraya eventually appeared, still attaching her earrings, and putting Raed's mind at ease that this might not have been a waste of time after all.

'It's a surprise and you look beautiful.'

'Not too much? I mean, if we're going for street food I can change into my jeans.' She gave a little twirl, letting him appreciate the gold sheath dress clinging to her curves and the matching shawl draped around her shoulders.

'You're perfect.' He held out his arm for her

to take as he escorted her outside to where a helicopter was waiting for them on the lawn.

'Raed? Dinner, you said, not a near-death experience,' she said, eyes wide as she took in the sight.

It hadn't occurred to Raed that the method of travel would prove a problem. He'd grown up used to being flown around at the drop of a hat to save time and avoid traffic and assumed Soraya would enjoy the same. Apparently he still had a lot to learn about how to impress her.

'I'm sorry. I didn't realise you would have an issue with flying.'

'A private jet with champagne on tap to soothe my fear of heights is one thing, but flying in one of those hamster balls is quite another ask.'

Raed's mood dipped. He knew he'd screwed up. They needed the chopper to get them to their destination in good time. If he had to change it now all of his plans would be disrupted.

'They're perfectly safe, I promise, and I can offer you all the champagne you wish when we land. But if you really don't want to go, I'll try and arrange something else.' He didn't want her to feel pressured into doing something she wasn't comfortable with when it would only end in disaster.

She looked at the helicopter and back at Raed. 'Is it far? I mean, maybe I could manage if it's not for long and you promise to hold my hand.'

'It's about a twenty-minute ride from here and I promise you can squeeze my hand the whole way there if it makes you feel better, but I don't want to force you into going.'

'No, I can do this. I suppose I'll have to get used to it as the next princess-to-be.' The sparkle in her eyes said Soraya's tongue was firmly in her cheek as she referenced her new royal role. It put a smile on his face. Which, frankly, given his personal circumstances recently, was a miracle.

Soraya took Raed's hand as they made their way to the helicopter. It had taken her a while to come to the decision that dinner was a good idea, but if she was all in with their pretend romance, then she had to play her part too. She assumed dinner would be some grand affair in public for maximum press exposure, given the palpitation-inducing suit he was wearing now.

Though she was dreading this trip with little to save them from plummeting to their deaths, she was already thinking about the feel of his hand in hers. The strength and comfort she drew from him was something she hadn't had for a long time and she wasn't sure she'd ever let go.

They climbed into the helicopter, Raed's bodyguard joining them, and the pilot up front who gave them a thumbs up. She had to remind herself this was the fake Soraya and Raed going to dinner, likely for a photo shoot, and not to be impressed that her rich boyfriend was flying her somewhere just for a meal.

'Are you okay? You can still change your mind if you want.' Raed gave her hand a squeeze as they settled into the seats of the helicopter. She appreciated that he was still giving her the option to back out even though he'd clearly gone to a lot of trouble to set this up.

'I'll be fine,' she lied, believing she could tough it out for twenty minutes if she really tried.

Then the blades started swishing, the sound obliterating any further conversation, and the chopper began to lift off the ground. She screwed her eyes tightly closed as the ground began to get farther and farther away, and clutched Raed's hand tighter.

After a little while, when she hadn't fallen out to her gruesome death, she began to loosen her grip. Raed tapped her on the shoulder and she felt brave enough to open her eyes again. He pointed out of the window, encouraging her to lean across to look out. The coloured lights from moving vehicles snaked their way through the streets, like arteries pumping life into the city now splayed out below them, the lights and movement of the traffic heralding the end of the working day as the sun set on the horizon outside the window, darkness claiming the skies.

For a moment it really began to feel as though they were escaping the pressure cooker their lives had become. She knew they'd be plunged back into the stress and hurly-burly of public life the moment they landed, but she had to accept the cons of this lifestyle if she wanted to enjoy the pros. For now she would take advantage of the respite, her nerves beginning to subside. Though she didn't let go of Raed's hand for the duration of their journey.

Eventually another pocket of tall buildings came into view, and when the helicopter came to rest on the roof of one, and the blades stopped whirring, she was finally able to relax.

'Where are you taking me?' she asked, slightly concerned that she had no idea where on earth they were. If he decided to ditch her now, or her very rational fear of crashing in that tiny flying bubble prevented her from making the return flight, she was in serious trouble in these heels.

'I told you, we're going to dinner.' Raed

jumped out of the helicopter and helped her out onto safer ground.

They were met by a small party of men and women in suits and chef outfits.

'Welcome, Your Royal Highness, and thank you for patronising our establishment tonight. Our chefs will prepare for you the very finest food we have to offer.'

The clearly awe-struck hosts bowed and curtseyed until Soraya was almost embarrassed by the display of gratitude. Raed of course took it all in his stride as he thanked the welcoming committee and added that they were ravenous after their journey. She didn't know if it was true or simply a ruse to get them to stop fawning but it did the trick as the party hustled back inside to prepare their food.

'How do you ever get used to that?' she asked Raed quietly as they made their way down into the restaurant via another recently renovated elevator.

'I never did, but it's part of the gig. People tend to lose their minds a bit when members of the royal family turn up, but I'm very lucky anyone still knows who I am in the current climate. I've lived quietly in London for some time but all of that has changed these past couple of days.'

Despite his obvious privilege, Raed somehow managed to stay humble and Soraya liked him even more for that. In her job she'd come across many surgeons at the top of their field who thought that gave them free rein to treat everyone else as though they were beneath them. That superiority complex wasn't attractive, but apparently a man who treated everyone with respect was someone she couldn't resist. It didn't bode well for however long they had to maintain this fake relationship when she was finding more reasons to fall for him.

'Wow.' It was the only thing she could manage to say when they walked into the restaurant, a circular room with full-size windows the whole way around. As it was beginning to get dark, candles were lit on each of the tables, still managing to give the place a cosy atmosphere. A lady dressed in a formal ball gown sat playing the piano with a harp sitting close by. The crystal chandeliers hanging all around were so numerous and heavy Soraya wondered how the ceiling stayed up, and the wall-to-wall white carpet and furnishings were a messy eater's nightmare. Even without the gold gilding on the walls the whole place screamed money. That part of her who'd struggled to buy even basic groceries after her parents had died baulked at the extravagance, but the new Soraya was enjoying this level of luxury. Raed was treating her to this decadent night out and it wouldn't hurt to indulge him when he was going to such lengths to impress her.

'We have reserved the best seat for you over here.' The maître d' bowed and led them over to a table for two at the window with impressive views over the city.

'Reserved? It's not exactly heaving with customers at the minute,' she whispered discreetly to Raed once they were alone, his security shadow seated at the bar where he could observe the room but wasn't close enough to hear their private conversation.

'I bought it out.'

'Pardon me?' Soraya spluttered on her glass of white wine.

Raed leaned across the table so the candlelight was dancing on his face. 'I covered what they would usually take for a full service tonight so we could be alone. No press, no gawkers, no pressure to be anyone but ourselves.'

Her mouth dropped open at the thought he would go to such lengths to make her feel comfortable. She wasn't sure she deserved it.

'Raed, it's really thoughtful of you but—'

'I know what you're going to say but I've come to an agreement with the restaurant that they will prepare all the meals they would usually cook over the evening and they're going to distribute them to local charities. Any excess produce will go to local foodbanks.' It was a move he knew she couldn't argue with.

'That's, that's, really generous of you.' She struggled to find words to express how grateful she was and was horrified to find tears pricking her eyes. It wouldn't do to launch into a sobbing fit, mascara running down her cheeks, her eyes and nose puffy and red, and ruin this beautiful moment. It was overwhelming.

'Now, what would you like to eat? I'm starving.' He snatched up the menu, scanning the extensive list for something to satisfy his hunger.

Soraya knew now there was only one thing—one man—who could satisfy hers, but unfortunately that wasn't on the menu.

Raed devoured his meal even though his stomach felt as though it would rebel at any moment with the thought of the next step he was about to take. They'd dined on lobster and mussels infused with saffron, and had lemon chiffon pie for dessert, every mouthful a taste experience.

'What's up, you stuffed too full of food to even talk now?' Soraya teased as she raised another forkful of lemon and cream to her lips.

He loved moments like this when they were just two people having dinner together, without outside pressures making them stressed or uncomfortable. There were no expectations other than enjoying one another's company, and that was easy as he genuinely liked being around Soraya. It was a shame they had all this other stuff circling around them, waiting for an opening to break through their happy bubble and spoil things. Perhaps it could wait a little longer.

'I was just thinking how nice this is. Normal. Well, except for the helicopter and the bodyguard and buying out the restaurant for some privacy.'

Soraya giggled. 'I've had a wonderful time, thank you.'

'If we weren't under so much scrutiny I'd take you to this place I love that makes the best chicken fajitas and margaritas. Mmm-mmm-mmm…' His mouth was watering for Mexican food, or anything that wasn't served up under a silver cloche with more cutlery than any one person could possibly use in one sitting. Since his family's troubles had begun he'd no longer been able to live his anonymous life, and had been absorbed back into the royal lifestyle.

'Like on a date, date? Sounds good to me.'

'It would be nice, wouldn't it? A meal, somewhere anonymous, a few drinks, then stroll home a little bit tipsy, with no need to worry about who's seen us.' As nice as this had been, it wasn't reality and never would be. However, it had been his decision to come back into the family fold, and he'd known what he was walking back into. He guessed now Soraya did too. It didn't make circumstances ideal.

She sighed. 'I don't know the last time I did that. Frank was always too busy with "work" for a date night. At least with me. For all I know, he was out on multiple dates when I stupidly believed he was staying late at the office trying to make a difference in the world. The only thing he managed to do was ruin my life.'

Soraya's playful tone had turned to something bitter and angry as she tossed back more of her wine. It was clear her break-up had been as devastating as his own, both experiencing a betrayal of sorts. Zara might not have cheated on him, or lied to him, but she hadn't stuck by him or even tried to make things work. She'd tossed their relationship away without even attempting to fight for it. He supposed he was guilty of doing the same, which ultimately proved that they hadn't been right for each other. From everything he'd heard about Frank he'd taken Soraya for granted and treated her despicably. Raed didn't want to be guilty of doing the same.

'Do you ever wonder what it would have been like if we'd met somewhere away from all this craziness? If we'd just been two surgeons who happened to cross each other's paths at a medical conference or a Mexican restaurant? When we weren't just getting over the breakdown of our relationships, obviously.' If he hadn't been so consumed with self-pity at the time they'd first met, they might actually have stood a chance.

Soraya thought for a moment before she responded.

'But we didn't, Raed. If there's one thing I've realised it's that there's no point in venturing down the "what if" route. Yeah, we might have met and perhaps there might have been something between us if we didn't have family to think about or a country to run, but that's not what happened. It's as pointless thinking that way as it is wondering how different life would have been if I'd been enough for Frank.' She hiccupped that last part of her monologue, the raw pain of her divorce still evident.

He'd been through that stage as well, blaming himself for how things had ended between him and Zara. It was only since meeting Soraya, having her support, that he'd begun to realise the failure of his relationship hadn't been entirely down to him, or Zara. This lifestyle hadn't been what either of them had signed up for and it simply hadn't been compatible with their relationship. If he'd been able to open his heart fully to her, perhaps she would have seen a future together, wherever that might have been. In Soraya's circumstances maybe if Frank hadn't spent so much time at work he wouldn't have succumbed to temptation. At the end of the day they'd simply been with the wrong people.

'Frank didn't appreciate the amazing woman he had waiting for him at home. That's not your fault. You're right, we shouldn't agonise over how things might have worked out if this or that hadn't happened. It won't change anything. We need to leave it all in the past where it belongs. Neither Zara nor Frank are part of our lives any more and I'm pretty sure neither of them are fretting about us right now. We have to move on.'

'I can't really do that yet though, can I? I mean, how do I move on when I'm here playing make-believe with a prince?' Her laugh had none of the usual warmth in it and Raed knew then that the real world had managed to pierce their illusion of normalcy already.

'I know we haven't made life easy with our ridiculous expectations of you, Soraya, but I do like to think all of this has helped you to move on emotionally at least.'

She eyed him with some scepticism.

'When you're mad at me, there isn't time to wallow in self-pity,' he explained with a grin.

'True, but you're not going to be around for ever, Raed.'

He wasn't sure if he'd imagined the fleeting look of sadness cloud her blue eyes, but he knew the time had come for him to make his next move.

'Then maybe we should make the most of our time together as our alter egos. If we're supposed to be engaged I thought we should make it official.' He felt for the ring box, which had been burning a hole in his pocket all night. While Soraya had been working this morning he'd made a special trip to an exclusive jeweller. Although the engagement wasn't real, what she'd done for his family was priceless and he wanted to show his appreciation to her with more than lip service.

He opened the box and held his breath, waiting for her reaction to the square-cut emerald on a diamond and platinum band. The frown across her forehead wasn't what he'd expected.

'I don't understand,' she said in the end.

'I thought it would complement your red hair.'

'But the engagement isn't real, why get a ring?'

'It'll look good in the photos,' he jested, but

she still wasn't smiling. 'Listen, we're going to have to make an official announcement, probably do a photo shoot. It's expected.'

'Oh, okay. It just seems…excessive.'

'I thought once all this is over that you could sell it or donate it to charity, or do anything you want with it.'

Her eyes widened. 'You're really giving this to me?'

'It's a token of my gratitude for everything you've done here. Really it's a two for one: it gets us some publicity and it could set you up with your new life.'

'Still—' She was staring at it as though she couldn't believe what she was seeing or hearing. It was down to Raed to take it out of its velvet cushion.

'Soraya Yarrow, will you do me the honour of becoming my fake fiancée?' It was an odd feeling proposing to someone he knew would never marry him.

After being with Zara for so long he'd felt that marriage would be their next logical step, part of life's plan. Not knowing it would come to an abrupt end a few years down the line. At least there were no expectations after this, only an impending feeling of loneliness once it was all over and Soraya went back to her old life.

'I made sure the stones were ethically sourced

too, so we both have a clear conscience over this at least.' He was sure the guilt over everything they were doing to protect his father and the reputation of the family as a whole would haunt him for some time to come. Along with dragging Soraya into the whole sordid affair.

She was admiring the emerald on her finger when the sound of a champagne cork reverberated around the room, followed by another procession of staff emerging from behind the scenes clapping and cheering.

'We're so honoured to have you here to celebrate your engagement.' The manager was beside himself with excitement, having apparently witnessed the royal engagement.

He glanced at Soraya, who was smiling uneasily at the gathered crowd. 'Thank you, but we're not ready to make a public announcement just yet. If you could hold off on telling anyone about this for now, we would be very grateful.'

'Of course, Your Royal Highness. Anything you want.' He gave a bow and while Raed was inclined to believe he was genuine about maintaining his silence on the matter for now, the same might not apply to the other members of staff present.

'If you can guarantee that this will stay between us, we will give details of tonight to the press with our announcement. I'm sure you'll have a rush of love-struck couples want-ing to come and have the same experience at your wonderful restaurant,' Soraya said, add-ing extra incentive for their co-operation, and though the official statement they would have to make was inevitable, this could give them a little longer to get used to the idea of their of-ficial relationship status.

'I promise my staff will be very discreet.' The now solemn-looking manager ushered his staff back towards the kitchen and Raed sus-pected they were going to have a stern talking-to about keeping their jobs to guarantee their silence.

'Very smooth. Perhaps you should take con-trol of our PR from now on,' he suggested, im-pressed with how she'd handled the situation.

'No, thanks. It's one thing reading rumours and gossip, but I don't think I'm prepared for the press descending en masse once we con-firm their suspicions. Still, it's what I signed up for, I guess, so I shouldn't complain.' Soraya stood up and wrapped her shawl around her shoulders, their night apparently at an end.

Even though they'd both decided it was pointless, Raed couldn't help but wish their circumstances had been different.

CHAPTER NINE

THE SHINE OF the evening had worn off for Soraya with the glint of that huge emerald. She knew she was being ungrateful when Raed had gifted it to her, not expecting to get it back when they inevitably called off their fake engagement. It was foolish of her to be upset that this had all been part of the greater PR plan.

Okay, so he'd tried to keep dinner as private as possible, and they'd had a lovely heart-to-heart about the wounds they were still carrying from their relationships. To her though, the reminder that this hadn't been a real date meant it ended on an unhappy note. It felt as if her emotions were being toyed with, especially after Raed had asked the question if they could've had something together if they'd met under different circumstances. Suggesting that he was interested in her, but knowing she would never be a viable option. It didn't help keep her emotions on lockdown believing there might have been more to that kiss between them than a publicity stunt after all. She wasn't an actress, or a celebrity with an alter ego—all of this toing and froing between playing his fiancée, and dealing with her real feelings for him, was causing havoc inside her.

Producing a ring to convince the wider public of their engagement was a reminder that none of this was real. But she'd made the decision to stay knowing all of this, so it was her own fault she was making herself miserable.

'Is everything all right, Soraya? You've been very quiet.' Raed helped her on with her seat belt before attending to his own.

'Sorry, I'm just tired,' she lied, not in the mood for small talk. At least, not until the helicopter started up again, and the nerves began to flutter in her belly.

'Is this thing okay to fly in the dark? How can he see where he's going?' She hated that she worried so much about things beyond her control, especially in front of Raed, who was so calm and taking everything in his stride, but to her mind these were legitimate concerns.

'Don't worry, he can see. You've flown in planes, right? It's the same principle. He has lights and radar and people to guide him if necessary. We're perfectly safe.' These were all things she knew in her heart but hearing him say them somehow made them more believable. Perhaps that was her problem—when Raed was being her charming fiancé for the cameras she was buying into the fantasy too. If he was able to lie to his country about major issues and pull the wool over their eyes, it wasn't a huge stretch to see why she would believe he was her doting other half even when she knew the stark truth.

She turned her head to look out of the window, away from temptation. Only for him to reach out and take her hand, pre-empting her need for his support. She didn't pull away, but it didn't help her predicament when he insisted on being nice to her away from the watching eyes of the world.

Suddenly, the relatively smooth journey back towards the palace took an unexpected turn. There was a loud bang and the helicopter lurched violently, lifting Soraya out of her seat before she was pulled back down by her restraints. Now, as the helicopter plunged down, taking her stomach with it, alarms were going off, and lights in the cockpit flashing, all as the pilot tried to wrestle some control. Even Raed looked concerned this time and that was reason enough for her to spiral, her pulse racing and heart lodged in her throat as panic set in.

'What's happening?'

'It's a bird strike,' the pilot relayed, though

it didn't allay her fears. Especially when she swore she could see a crack in the windshield.

'What does that mean?'

'Usually it means there's been a collision with a bird, or even a flock of them. I'm sure they'll let us know if it's anything serious.' Raed smiled and squeezed her hand, presumably to convince her she was still safe. However, his reassurances couldn't drown out the chaos happening all around them.

'You're going to have to brace yourselves back there. We need to land and we're coming in hard. The damage is too great for us to stay in the air. I've radioed for help but strap yourselves in, this is going to be a bumpy one. I'm going to try and head for some waste ground, away from more populated areas.'

The pilot's update prompted Raed to check their belts again. 'We'll ride this one out together. I'm here for you.' He lifted her hand to his mouth and kissed it.

Soraya closed her eyes as the helicopter descended rapidly, too quickly for her to catch her breath.

There was so much noise her head felt as though it were going to explode. People shouting, the mechanical sound of the helicopter struggling to fly, alarms blaring, and her heart pounding.

'Mayday, mayday.'

That high-pitched squeal she assumed was the helicopter in freefall grew louder as her stomach lurched. Anything not bolted down was being tossed around inside adding to the sense of chaos, and all the time Raed was clutching her hand.

'We're going to die.' Her voice was remarkably calm, as though she'd simply accepted that this was the end for them.

'Not if I can help it,' Raed told her, jaw clenched, fingers tightly wrapped around hers, and Soraya loved him for his determination, no matter how futile.

Suddenly she needed to tell him that. 'I'm not sure you can but thank you for looking after me. If we do die—'

'But we're not going to,' Raed interrupted as the helicopter jolted again, making a mockery of his words.

'If we do…' Soraya had to shout to be heard over the din of their impending crash '… I want you to know I would have done this without the money for the centre. I… I like being with you, Raed. Even though you drive me crazy at times, and I know it could never work out between us, not least because we're about to die in a ball of flames…'

Before she could descend into complete

panic, Raed silenced her with a hard kiss. His lips were insistent and demanding on hers, as though he was trying to make up for lost time. Soraya screwed her eyes shut, trying to block out the crisis going on around them and focus on the feel of Raed against her. She gripped him by the lapels of his jacket, and pulled him as close as the seat belt would bring him, kissing him back. Completely in freefall, body and soul.

Eventually they had to break apart as gravity and the intensity of the moment stole away their breath. Soraya tried to brace herself for the inevitable crash but one look at Raed and she was putty again. Those soulful brown eyes were locked onto hers and if it was the last image she ever saw she'd die happy.

'I don't think I'd have had the strength to come back if I hadn't had you by my side,' he said, making her heart melt. 'Just in case I never get to say it again, I'm glad I have you in my life.'

Tears filled Soraya's eyes with the unfairness of it all. She knew they were only saying these things to one another because they were staring death in the face. It was cruel irony to find out now he did reciprocate her feelings when they were never going to get a chance to do anything about it. If they'd been braver, willing to face their demons when they weren't in a life-or-death situation, there could have been more kissing, more Raed, more everything. Now they were facing the end of it all.

The embrace they shared in that moment was an attempt to cling onto life just a little bit longer, holding each other so tightly she never wanted to let go.

They were plummeting, the cacophony of sound around them overwhelming.

'Just hold on,' Raed shouted above the noise, then he covered her body with his like a protective shell as they hit the ground with a deafening crunch.

Soraya's head whipped back and forward with the impact and she lifted out of her seat before being thrust back into it. They seemed to skid along the ground for some time before the interior of the helicopter was filled with dust and dirt. Only then did she open her eyes and try to move, all to no avail. It was pitch black and she had a heavy weight pressing her down. She felt around to try and figure out what had landed on her and her hands found Raed still shielding her body with his.

'Raed,' she croaked, her lips dry, her throat parched.

When he didn't respond she nearly stopped breathing herself, afraid that he mightn't ever wake up again. The thought was so devastating she didn't want to contemplate it for another second. She couldn't lose him when they'd just confessed their feelings for one another.

'Raed, wake up,' she said more urgently, shaking him and praying for signs of life.

He gave a groan and gradually the weight lifted from her body as he sat up. Relief helped to settle her heart back into an almost normal rhythm.

'Soraya? Are you okay?'

She was touched that his first thought was for her even though he was the one who'd struggled to wake up. It spoke of feelings for her that went beyond her being a mere convenience to him, and, though that brought its own problems, for now she needed it. After opening herself up, admitting that she more than liked him, it was reassuring to know that he hadn't simply said those words to her because he thought he was dying. It was an even playing field now they'd both confessed.

'Yeah. A bit banged up but I'll live. Thanks to you. Are you all right?' It was hard to see him in the dark and check for injuries, so she had to rely on him to tell her if he was hurt. He'd been so intent on protecting her she doubted he would even say if he had a leg hanging off, so as not to upset her.

'A few cuts and bruises. I think I got hit by some of the debris. That'll teach me to leave water bottles lying around.' He was still trying to make her smile, even in the wake of a horrible crash that had knocked him unconscious.

Soraya couldn't stop the sob that had bubbled up from nowhere and erupted into the quiet night, the seriousness of what had just happened suddenly catching up with her. Not to mention the thoughts of an alternative, and very final, ending. In the face of death, her life hadn't flashed before her. Her thoughts had been only of Raed and wanting to be with him. A serious development that complicated everything about their fake engagement, but, with no time to overthink, her real feelings had come to the fore. In that moment the fact that they'd be living in two different countries, that he had other priorities than her, wasn't an issue. The only thing that mattered was that he was safe.

'Hey, it's going to be all right. The pilot radioed for help and the emergency services won't be far behind. Everything's going to be okay.' He brushed her hair tenderly away from the stream of tears now flooding down her face. It only made her cry harder.

'You said that before the crash.' She hiccupped.

Raed sighed. 'I know, I'm sorry. The birds

must've hit the propeller blades and caused us to spin out of control. It's very rare, especially at this time of night. We were very unlucky, but, hey, we're both alive to tell the tale.'

'I thought you were dead.' Soraya couldn't help the renewed torrent of tears, imagining what could have happened.

'Well, I'm not.'

'So why can't I stop crying?' She was laughing at herself through her tears because Raed made it so easy for her not to be scared even though they were sitting in wreckage goodness knew where in the outskirts of the city. There was no way of knowing what was in store for them next, or if their earlier revelations would come to anything, but she was relieved Raed was still here with her.

'It's shock. We've just been involved in a major trauma. Mine will probably hit later but for now I'm more concerned with getting out of here in case there's a fuel leak somewhere.' Raed was right, they probably had a lot to discuss, but for now they had to concentrate on their safety.

'What about the others?' she asked as he wrestled to get the jammed seat belts off both of them.

'Let me get you to a safe distance, then I'll come back and check on the others.'

Soraya gave him the side eye. 'You know that's not going to happen.'

She heard him take in a breath, as though he was about to argue then he realised it was pointless.

'I just don't want you getting hurt.' He paused the struggle with the belt to rethink his words. 'Sorry. I don't mean to patronise you, you're every bit as capable as I am. All I want is to keep you safe.'

'I know.' How could she be mad at him when his intentions were so honourable? Despite the horrendous situation they'd ended up in, it was nice to have someone to look out for her for a change. Someone who'd protected her with his body, his life, as they'd crashed. She would never forget that.

In the end he had to lift up the fabric of the belt while she wiggled her way out. It was only then she realised she must have been bumped around more than she'd thought, her hip bones aching when she brushed against anything.

They stepped cautiously over the detritus now littering the floor to get into the cockpit where both the pilot and bodyguard were unconscious. The windscreen was shattered, glass and blood covering everything.

'I'll see to Steve. He seems the most badly

hurt. Can you see to Duke?' Raed climbed in beside the pilot, who was slumped against what was left of the blood-smeared window, not hesitating to enlist her medical expertise.

She set to work assessing the bodyguard.

'He's tachycardic. Breathing shallow. Signs of cyanosis. Suspected pneumothorax.' The fast pulse combined with the blue tinge of his skin suggested he'd suffered a collapsed lung, perhaps caused by a fracture of the ribs during impact.

'Steve's breathing and has a steady pulse. Let me go look for some first-aid supplies.'

The sound of Raed banging around in the wreckage gave her some comfort knowing he was close by. It was going to be difficult returning to a life where she was the one who carried everyone else's worries and expectations on her shoulders. At least here she had Raed to turn to, to share her fears, her problems, and emergency medical situations. She hoped she did the same for him when he had the weight of an entire kingdom wearing him down. By agreeing to stay and keep the myth of their relationship alive, she was relieving him of some of that burden. Even if maintaining the pretence and attempting to keep their personal lives separate from their public personas brought different issues.

'There's a good first-aid kit, probably in case of emergencies like this, and some blankets. Along with this because you're shivering.' Raed emerged with an armful of supplies and what was left of her gold wrap. He carefully draped it around her shoulders.

A sudden rush of love at the gesture, that even in the midst of this disaster he was thinking of her, threatened to overwhelm her. She managed to swallow down her emotions to focus on treating their patient because now wasn't the time for that kind of epiphany. If she let herself think about the fact she'd fallen completely for a prince she'd start to catastrophise the situation even more. At least when they'd thought they were going to die they hadn't had time to overthink, only express how they felt about one another, and that wasn't something she was going to forget in a hurry.

'Thank you,' she said, accepting the gesture without spiralling about all the reasons they shouldn't be together.

Later, when they were somewhere safe and private, they could deal with the new emotional development between them, but for now there were other issues at hand. As medics, in this emergency situation, they had to put other people's welfare before their own personal issues.

'We should probably get him out of here,' Raed concluded.

'Yeah, I really don't like his colour. With no sign of the emergency services, I think I'm going to have to do a needle decompression.' Duke's rapid deterioration was likely attributed to chest trauma trapping air in his pleural cavity. If left untreated it could lead to cardiac arrest. They needed to release the trapped air.

Raed manoeuvred himself in behind Duke and lifted him under the arms, leaving Soraya to grab his legs. Between them they managed to carry him out of the cockpit and set him down on the ground outside. Soraya quickly opened Duke's shirt, noted the severe bruising to his chest and listened to his breathing using a stethoscope from the medical bag Raed had salvaged.

'Decreased breath sounds suggesting a partially collapsed lung,' she confirmed.

Without hesitation Raed opened a new needle and handed it to her. It showed his confidence in her and her abilities once again and Soraya liked that he wasn't the kind of arrogant man who tried to take over, or thought he knew best. He trusted her, and she knew that wasn't something he gave away easily when he took on so many responsibilities for himself.

She used a sterile wipe to clean Duke's chest,

and felt along for the second intercostal space along the mid-clavicular line.

'Where's Amir when you need him?' she joked, as the implications of getting this wrong hovered in her psyche. As a thoracic surgeon, Raed's brother was the one who performed this procedure on a regular basis, but Soraya was acutely aware in this moment of the things that could go wrong. If she failed to penetrate the wall, or damaged any of the organs, she could make Duke's situation worse.

'You can do this,' Raed assured her, and she knew he was right.

Just above the third rib, she plunged the needle into the chest at a ninety-degree angle and was rewarded with the hissing sound of air escaping. She removed the needle, leaving the catheter to keep the airway open, and taped it in place. Only once she was finished did she take a shaky breath of relief.

'One down, one to go,' she said with a smile, aware that this wasn't over yet. They still had another patient waiting for their assistance.

'I can get Steve…you stay here with Duke. I think you've done your part.' Raed covered both Soraya and Duke with blankets, then dropped a kiss on her forehead before going back to retrieve the pilot.

It was this kind of teamwork, looking out for

each other, that she enjoyed, and was going to miss most when their fake romance came to an end. Despite all their differences, he treated her as an equal, not a fool to be duped and used as Frank had done. She was beginning to hope there was some way to continue their relationship, because she didn't want to go back to a life without that support, without Raed.

She watched as Raed grabbed hold of Steve's shoulders and began to drag him from his seat. He managed to get him halfway out of the helicopter and onto the ground, but there was clearly something wedging his feet and preventing him from getting out. Soraya realised it wouldn't be an easy task for him to manage alone. It wasn't in her nature to simply stand back and watch someone struggle so she rushed over and offered another pair of hands.

'I've got him. You see what has trapped him in there.' Soraya bent down and covered him with her blanket. Whatever other injuries he had, she didn't want him going into shock as well. Keeping his body temperature regulated would help prevent that.

'Uh, Soraya, we have a situation here.' Raed motioned her over to where he'd been pulling out bits of mangled machinery in an attempt to dislodge the man's lower half.

When she peeked inside, where Raed was using the torch on his phone to light the interior, she had to cover her mouth to stave off the sudden urge to vomit.

Even though she was a trained, experienced surgeon, the sight that met her was hard to stomach. The foot, still encased in the shoe, was barely attached to the rest of the leg, bone visible and turned the wrong way around.

'Can you get him out?' Preferably without accidentally amputating the foot.

'I can now, but we're going to have to be very careful. I'm sorry but I'm going to need you to hold the foot in place while I try to manoeuvre him out of here.'

Soraya had to push through the nausea and squeamishness to focus on their patient and saving his foot. It would be career-ending, or at the very least life-altering, for him to lose it. She and Raed were both used to saving lives in difficult circumstances and this shouldn't be any different, even though they didn't have the comfort or the facilities of a modern hospital. The amount of food she had eaten for dinner, however, was coming back to haunt her.

'No problem.' She ducked inside the door and leaned down so she could reach the foot, turning it to where it should have been and holding it firmly in place as Raed gently eased

Steve's legs out onto the ground, bringing her with them.

Afraid to set the open wound down and risk infection from dirt and sand getting in there, she rested the foot on her lap. Raed grabbed bandages and dressings from the medical supplies.

'This should keep the foot in place until help arrives.'

'Any word on that?' she grumbled. The longer they were all stuck here, the greater they were at risk of something happening to them too. She would have expected a search party out here the second this precious prince disappeared. Even though it had been mere minutes since they'd crashed it already felt like an eternity.

'They will be here as soon as they can. They're probably just trying to pinpoint exactly where we've come down. The best thing we can do is have him ready to transport the second they get here. Okay?' He nodded towards their injured companion and she knew he was right. If anything they were lucky Raed had been part of this, because they'd pull out all the stops to find him, not write them off as missing presumed dead.

Soraya kept talking to her patient, though he was still unresponsive. Currently it wasn't such a bad thing he was sleeping through the pain, but she hoped he hadn't suffered any head injuries she hadn't spotted, or internal bleeding that could cause complications to his recovery.

'Okay, we need to get that bone in place again, then we'll strap it up. Hopefully at the hospital they can operate and repair the damaged muscle and tendons so he can maintain mobility.' It was all they could do on this end as well as try to keep the blood circulation going for now.

Soraya tried again to rouse their patient, or at least find out if he was awake, while they attempted to push the bone back in place. The last thing she wanted was for him to suddenly kick out in pain and damage himself or them.

When there was no response they agreed to forge ahead. She gently lifted the foot from her lap and Raed held the end of the leg securely.

'One, two, three—' They counted together and on three she forced the two pieces of exposed bone back together.

Raed began strapping the foot and leg to keep it in place. He spread one blanket on the ground and covered the patient with another. Once she was sure the foot had been stabilised Soraya was able to rest the whole leg on the blanket so she could stand up and stretch hers.

'Good job.' He high-fived her and it made

her smile after the stress and tension of the last few minutes.

In an operating theatre she had some control over what happened, was able to work with the benefit of X-rays and cameras to assist her. Here in the dark, working solely on their instincts, with these men's lives at stake, there was a question mark hanging over what they were doing. And if it was good enough. That uncertainty wasn't something she could shake off easily.

It was only when she looked back at the crash site Soraya realised how lucky they had been to be able to walk away. The tail was completely severed from the rest of the helicopter, taking the brunt of the hit, she supposed, as the pilot did his best to land in the field. If they had hit anything other than this grassy oasis she was sure none of them would have survived the impact.

Thankfully the sound of rotor blades were heard in the skies above them, followed by a bright search light from the rescue helicopter scanning the area around them.

'We're down here.' Regardless that they probably couldn't hear her, Soraya was yelling at the search party and waving her wrap high above her head in an attempt to catch their attention.

It was such a relief that help had arrived, but there was still that fragment of doubt lingering in her anxious thoughts that they would somehow be missed. Even the regal Raed was flagging them down with both hands high in the air, yelling at them like any other stranded, traumatised civilian desperate to be saved.

They waited impatiently until the helicopter found somewhere to land, followed by the arrival of an ambulance a few minutes later. A team of paramedics rushed straight to Raed, but he dismissed their concerns and directed them towards Soraya and the two men.

'I'm fine,' she insisted as one of the medical crew veered over to see her.

'You should really get checked out at the hospital. We've been running on adrenaline since the crash and who knows what injuries might be hiding?' Raed said as he came to join her.

'I will if you will,' she said, more concerned with the possible injuries Raed could have sustained while he'd been shielding her. It would also give her a chance to get an update on their patients and their future prognosis.

There was little else they could do at this point, but it didn't make it any easier to walk away. They were chivvied into an ambulance and Raed took her hand.

'I know it's tough. It's not in our nature to

walk away from our patients, but we will be diverting to the hospital where they're being transferred.'

The farther they left the scene behind, the more Soraya noticed her breath was becoming shallower by the second. She closed her eyes and tried to regulate it, squeezing Raed's hand so tightly it was even hurting her. Whatever it took to get her mind off the accident.

'Next time we'll get the driver to take us somewhere local for dinner.' Raed's lame attempt at humour at least managed to distract her from the vision in her head of the ground rushing up to meet them again long enough to roll her eyes at him.

'I'll settle for a takeaway, thanks.' She almost managed a smile, then she looked into his eyes and saw the same ghost of the horror they'd just experienced haunting him too. Without thinking about anything other than the need to comfort him, and feel his warmth against her, Soraya launched herself at him and swamped Raed in a hug.

She could feel the initial surprise in the tension of his body, then he relaxed, tightened his hold around her and buried his head in her neck. They sat that way for some time, oblivious to the others around them, concerned only with the comfort they were drawing from one another, it seemed.

'You smell of diesel and dirt,' he whispered into her ear to make her laugh even when all she wanted to do was cry.

'You say the sweetest things,' she mumbled back, even though it was exactly the right thing to say in the moment. If he'd apologised for the events that had been out of everyone's control, or said anything remotely nice, it would have made her over-emotional. She was barely holding it together.

'We'll be at the hospital soon.'

She didn't know who'd said it, but it was the reason Raed had moved away from her. He sat back in his seat and before that bereft feeling chilled her again, he pulled her into his chest. She nestled against him with a sigh, in too great a need for his support to concern herself with the consequences of being so close to him. There would be time for self-recrimination later, but for now she needed this, needed Raed.

CHAPTER TEN

RAED AND SORAYA barely made it through the palace doors before their phones were ringing.

'We were so afraid you'd been hurt when they said your helicopter had gone down, Raed.'

'Don't ever do that to me again, sis.'

It seemed their families had joined together upon hearing the news. On speaker phone, his mother and Soraya's sister immediately let them know how worried they'd been about them even though he knew they'd been informed they were safe the second the search party had found them. He understood. There'd been times when he'd thought they mightn't make it too. His first and only thought when it was apparent the helicopter was going down had been to protect Soraya.

Protocol and common sense, when his father wasn't in good health and he was next in line to the throne, should have dictated he got himself to safety at all costs. However, his heart had reacted first, and he would have willingly given his life to save hers.

It was only the luck of his birth that had bestowed this status and wealth upon him, Soraya was a better person than he could ever hope to be. She'd never lied to anyone or shunned her family even when she'd been left in the most difficult circumstances. But above all of that, deep down he knew it was his feelings for her that had made him act so recklessly.

Soraya's welfare had suddenly become more important to him than his other responsibilities and that was remarkable given the task he currently had keeping the country running in his father's absence.

Even now, as they were having their ears assaulted by well-meaning family members, his instinct was to carry her off somewhere private to give her some space to decompress.

They'd both been through a lot tonight and if she was feeling anywhere near what he was experiencing, she needed time out too.

'Did you get checked out at the hospital?' Amir asked, the concern evident in his tone.

'We're fine, brother. Just a few cuts and bruises. Duke and Steve are both in surgery, but it looks as though they're going to be all right. If you don't mind we'll talk you all through it tomorrow.' Their families had been understandably worried and upset but he thought it was too much to deal with their feelings on top of their own. They had a lot to process.

'Raed's right. We're fine, everybody. I really just want to have a shower and go to bed.' Soraya shut down his plans to spend some downtime together but at least she would be getting some rest. He would do the same, if his mind would calm sufficiently to let him sleep.

'Okay. I'll give you some space.' Her sister sounded a little put out but thankfully she agreed to Soraya's wishes.

'It's been a long night. Thanks, everyone.' He hung up and escorted Soraya up to her room.

'I want to thank you for everything you did for me tonight,' she said outside her door.

'What? Nearly get you killed in a helicopter crash?' He was only half joking about that, and it would be a long time before he forgave himself for putting her in that situation. It wasn't going to do anything for her fear of flying.

'It wasn't your fault and I don't want you beating yourself up over it. I was talking about the way you protected me.' She smiled at him, her bottom lip quivering, her eyes shimmering with unshed tears. It was clear she needed some time on her own, but he was reluctant to leave her now.

'I just wanted to make sure you were okay.

I still do.' He waited for her to say she wanted him to stay, but when she didn't he knew it was time to leave.

After everything they'd been through tonight, the feelings they'd admitted to in the heat of the moment, there was a lot for them to discuss but she obviously wasn't ready for it. If it meant facing the fact that she had to go home because a relationship between them simply wasn't viable, then neither was he.

'You know where I am if you need someone to talk to later,' he said before walking away. He only took a few steps before he had the urge to turn back again. 'You were amazing tonight with Duke and Steve. I hope you know that.'

'Just doing my job,' she said with a smile, but they both knew it was so much more than that.

He knew at the hospital she had a good reputation, that was why he'd wanted her to perform his father's operation and give him the best possible chance of surviving. Being out there tonight in such adverse conditions proved what an amazing woman she was, brave and skilful, and always doing her best for those around her.

Soraya was the only person he could turn to, who understood him at the best of times. After everything they'd gone through tonight, something no one else would be able to comprehend, he could use some time to talk things through with her. To work out what they were going to do about this connection they had between them. They couldn't ignore it when they'd spent the aftermath of the tragedy in each other's arms blocking out the rest of the world.

He didn't know what they were going to do about it when they both had their own lives to go back to once this fake engagement was over and his father was back in his rightful place. But ignoring their feelings wasn't going to make life any easier for them and was storing up trouble for the future. Perhaps they needed to call a halt to the whole thing now before they were in so deep they couldn't walk away without sustaining serious injuries, or maybe they could actually try making a go of this relationship they were alleged to be in already.

If Soraya agreed to a fling for the duration of her stay, before her return home, they might be able to walk away at the end of this without regrets. In his experience so far, she wouldn't want to remain in this environment long term, so he knew an actual relationship was heartache waiting to happen. However, if they embarked on some no-strings time together they could let this chemistry fizz itself out, minus the recriminations at the end of it. They could enjoy the initial passion of that attraction finally sparking to life, and get out before there was nothing left but ashes of the people they once used to be. At least they would both know going into it that 'till death do us part' was never going to be an option. It was lies anyway. Everyone always abandoned him, at least this way he had some control over how and when it would happen.

There was no way of knowing if this was something Soraya would contemplate since she wasn't ready to talk to him. Until then he'd just have to drive himself crazy thinking about her.

The night had started out with such promise and hope, and almost ended in tragedy. He didn't want the same to happen to him and Soraya. Raed hoped she would seek him out at some point. As much for his sake as her own.

Soraya turned on the shower and stepped under the spray, letting the hot water soothe her weary body. The next best thing to having Raed's arms around her.

She'd needed him to hold her tonight, getting used to having him there for her in a crisis. It wasn't something she'd had in her life before, always the one her parents, her sister, and even Frank had turned to when they'd needed support. Usually she ploughed on through life carrying her burdens alone, dealing with them behind the scenes so as not to upset anyone.

It was different with Raed. In him she had a confidant she could share her troubles with, or simply lean on when she needed to be held.

She thought of the way he'd wrapped her body up in his as the helicopter had gone down, putting his life on the line to protect her. Frank would never have done anything as selfless as that for her. For the duration of their marriage she was the one who'd taken care of bills so he didn't stress about money, and done everything she could to make his life comfortable. He'd never done the same for her.

She wondered if he'd ever truly loved her, or if she'd simply been a soft touch he'd taken advantage of. Using her generous nature to fund whatever, or whoever, he fancied. He'd never contributed financially and she'd excused it as he'd been working for the greater good of the community. Allegedly. When it had come to their marriage she'd been the one to put the effort in, making their house a home, cooking dinners, or arranging date nights. Looking back, she'd put up with it because she'd been so invested in their relationship, trying to force it to work because she'd thought she'd left it too late to ever find anyone else to love her. Ha!

She would have been better off on her own than being married to a liar and a cheat.

Frank would have avoided her at times like

this, unable to deal with any display of emotion, waiting for her to 'get over it'. Not Raed, who was encouraging her to talk to him, letting her know it was okay to feel the way she did. She was so used to holding everything back, to bottling up her emotions to protect everyone else, she was afraid to pop the cork and pour them out.

For all the struggles they'd encountered tonight, the worst of all was that moment of believing she'd lost Raed for ever. He'd brought so much into her life she couldn't bear the thought of no longer having him in it. It was then she realised that she loved him. Despite all the pitfalls that would surely arise, she'd failed to prevent it.

She closed her eyes, dipped her head under the stream of water, and cried out all of her fears, her upset, and all the uncertainty the future held. Her tears mixed with the warm water, cleansing her skin and her soul at the same time.

When she was all cried out, and her skin was beginning to prune, she dried herself off and put her pyjamas on for bed.

Even thoughts of Raed, the way he'd wrapped himself around her, put her needs above his own, wouldn't settle her, because she knew she should be with him now. It was fear keeping her from him, that acting on this attraction would somehow make her life worse. But Raed had helped to pick her back up again after Frank's betrayal and given her security where she'd had none. It mightn't last for ever if they did embark on a relationship, but, as tonight had proved, nothing in this life was guaranteed. She owed it to herself to at least see if there was something worth exploring with Raed, even for a short while. It was time to put her needs first for once.

Raed couldn't sleep. Not when he was worried about how Soraya was coping with everything. The emotional shock that occurred after such a traumatic event wasn't something she should be going through on her own.

It was a relief when he heard the knock on his door and he saw her standing outside.

'Soraya? What's wrong?' He knew there had to be something serious enough to bring her to him at this hour and he could tell by the redness around her eyes that she'd been crying.

She bounced up on her tiptoes and wrapped her arms around his neck. Her mouth demanded a response from his and she got it, his whole body coming alive at the touch of her against him again.

'I thought maybe, you know, we could give this thing a shot. At least until…'

'You have to go home,' he continued, dragging her into his room and kicking the door shut behind her.

Now they were both on the same page that this was a temporary arrangement, that it shouldn't interfere with their lives beyond her stay, it felt as though they were making up for lost time. Their mouths and tongues were seeking each other out, desperate to make that same connection they'd had in the car park that day. The passion hadn't lessened in the interim.

Raed had his hands on her backside as they stumbled into his bedroom, and she was letting hers roam through his hair, down his chest, wherever she could touch him. His whole body was on fire for her, burning with a restlessness to have her completely.

He slipped her robe from her shoulders, kissing the silky skin as he uncovered it, enjoying her gasp when he nibbled the skin at the crook of her neck. Slowly, he slid the spaghetti straps of her camisole down her arms, revealing her full breasts to his hungry gaze and mouth. When he dipped his head to claim her nipple with his mouth, Soraya writhed against him, her hands tugging his hair.

'Is this okay? I don't want to do something

you'll regret tomorrow. You've had a shock and I know emotions are running high.' As much as he wanted this, he had to be sure this wasn't some knee-jerk reaction to their near-death experience tonight. He wanted her to do this for all the right reasons, to enjoy this as much as he did.

'Don't. Stop,' she said, her breathy voice heavy with desire, telling him everything he needed to know.

He dropped to his knees and cupped her breasts in his hands, kneading, sucking, worshipping her beautiful body.

'Raed,' she pleaded when he nudged her legs apart and drew her silk shorts torturously slowly down her body, delaying the moment of satisfaction for both of them.

When she was fully exposed to him, he buried his face between her soft thighs and parted her with his tongue. He felt her knees buckle, her fingers tighten in his hair, and heard her groan. All the encouragement he needed to delve deeper inside her.

With his hands firmly planted on her backside, he tasted and teased that most intimate part of her until they were both fit to burst. Her moans of pleasure gradually increased, her breath ragged, as he brought her to the edge of ecstasy, then tipped her right over. She was clutching at his head, her legs shaking, her cry echoing around the room as she climaxed at the tip of his tongue. Only when the ripples of her orgasm finally subsided, the tension leaving her body, did he relent in his pursuit.

He took her hand and led her towards the bed where they lay side by side, staring into one another's eyes. Her cheeks were flushed, her pupils dark, and her lips swollen. She was beautiful.

'When we're in this room, the outside world doesn't exist, okay?' He didn't want anything to spoil this. Here they could pretend this was all they needed. Each other.

'Fine by me.' She smiled, invitation enough for him to kiss her again.

He was glad she'd come to him of her own volition, that he hadn't had to convince her this was a good idea. It meant she was as powerless to control this thing as he was and now they didn't have to, all bets were off. There was no holding back.

With more time to explore one another, the kisses were long and tender, satisfying and loving.

'I could stay here for ever.' His defences down, the words slipped out. Thankfully Soraya didn't laugh, or freeze, the moment over. Instead, apparently in agreement, she reached for him.

'Tonight will have to do.' She leaned in to kiss him, letting her hand stroke his erection through his boxer briefs.

That light touch was enough to steal his breath and only make him want her more. He pulled off his underwear, eager to feel her hands on him. This time she gripped him tightly, taking possession of him that he willingly gave. She moved her hand up and down his shaft, making it easy for him to relax and let her take control of his body when it felt so good.

Except he wanted more of Soraya, he needed all of her.

He rolled over so his body was pressed firmly against hers, took that sweet pink nipple in his mouth again, and she arched her hips up into his. As tempted as he was to take her there and then, pregnancy was a complication they couldn't afford. That wasn't part of a no-strings deal. So he reached into his nightstand for a condom and sheathed himself quickly.

When he did finally drive into Soraya's warmth, joining them together for the first time, he hoped it wouldn't be the last.

Soraya gasped as Raed filled her, but she was ready for him, ready for this. They wouldn't have this time together for long and she didn't want to waste any more of it. Especially when he was making so much effort to please her.

She sucked in a deep breath as he grazed her nipple with his teeth and thrust inside her again. Her whole body was tingling with arousal and wanting, and she couldn't get enough of him.

Sex with Frank had been perfunctory at best, and infrequent near the end of their marriage. Perhaps that had been the cause of his infidelity, not a result. It didn't excuse any of his behaviour but she was beginning to see their marriage completely differently now, since meeting Raed. They'd never had this passion, this chemistry, this animal lust for one another, and she'd thought that was okay. That she simply wasn't a passionate woman, or someone who inspired it in a man. Frank hadn't been her first, but she hadn't been with anyone else particularly memorable either. She'd assumed her late start in the dating pool meant she'd missed out on the fun part of sex, that she'd been too old to enjoy it. That whatever was wrong in her love life was down to her. Now she realised she simply hadn't been with the right person.

It made all the difference wanting someone so bad she couldn't think straight, and knowing he felt the same made her glow from the inside out. Perhaps it was the holding back that made this all the more explosive and exciting.

All the secrecy and lies had been stressful, but being with him tonight felt like the ultimate release. Something that might not be sustained long term, but, given that they'd agreed on a fling, hopefully she could enjoy this level of passion for the duration of her stay at least. It was going to be difficult to leave him, to leave this feeling of absolute ecstasy behind, but at least she would have the memories. And the truth that there was nothing wrong with her. It had taken Raed to show that to her.

When he was kissing her the way he was right now, making love to her so tenderly and passionately, she felt like the only person in the world. As though she were the centre of his world. Even though it might not be true, it was the first time she'd ever felt like that. It was intoxicating, and she wanted him to experience it too.

She tightened her inner muscles around him, heard the hitch in his breath as he fought for restraint, and saw the smile on his lips before he resumed control. He plunged inside her again and again, until she forgot she was supposed to be the one driving him crazy. Carried away on that floaty feeling of bliss, she cried out as she reached nirvana, her orgasm catching her by surprise.

Only when she slowly drifted back into her

body again did she blink her eyes open, woozy from her out-of-body experience.

'There you are.' Raed was staring down at her, his expression so full of love and desire for her in that moment it made her want to weep. 'I wondered where you'd gone.'

'You know exactly where I went,' she said with a coy smile.

'Well, I'm glad you're back with me now.' He resumed kissing her neck, moving his hips against hers, and joining them together again.

It wasn't long before he took his own trip to that thought-stealing, brain-scrambling place of wonder as he announced his climax with a caveman-like roar. The sound of him losing control brought a smile of satisfaction to her lips. It matched the one he wore when he came to lie down beside her again on the bed.

'Tell me again why we didn't do this sooner?' he asked through panting breaths as he struggled to recover.

'Er…because you were rude and unreachable when we first met,' she reminded him.

'And broken-hearted, if you remember.'

'Hmm.'

'But I'm over that now.' He reached across and gave her a long, leisurely kiss that her body responded to as though it wasn't completely exhausted by his physical attentions already.

'Me too.' Soraya meant it. Even before to-night, she'd come to terms with what had happened between her and Frank. Raed had been the one to help her move on and she was grateful for the time they had together, even if it wasn't going to last for ever.

'Hey. You disappeared again. Only this time it doesn't look as though it was to a happy place.' Raed tilted her chin up so she had to look at him, no doubt the pain she was feeling at the thought of losing him again written across her face.

'I was just thinking about when I have to leave.'

'It's not for a while yet. Let's just enjoy what we have until then.' He cuddled her close, muffled her worries with his warm body, and kept her distracted for the rest of the night.

Yet, when dawn broke and they had to leave the cocoon they'd made in his bed, it was the only thing she could think of.

CHAPTER ELEVEN

'I'D LIKE TO go and visit Steve and Duke at the hospital. Do you think that's possible?' Soraya asked as they ate breakfast in bed.

The news of their 'engagement' last night in the restaurant, along with tales of their 'heroics' at the crash scene, had been all over the news by the time they'd woken so he hadn't seen any point in smuggling her back to her own room to save face in front of palace staff. As far as the country was concerned they were a real couple so it shouldn't come as any shock that they'd spent the night together.

'Sure. I'll put in a call for the car and security detail while you get ready. As gorgeous as you are naked with bedhead and a post-coital glow, I'm sure it's not the image you want captured the moment we set foot outside the palace.'

Now the palace had made the official announcement to coincide with the leaked pictures from the restaurant last night—someone

was definitely getting the sack over that one—
Raed knew all hell was about to break loose.
Public interest would be through the roof to
find out all the details about him and his new
fiancée. While that had been the plan all along,
to divert attention away from the real story of
his father's heart problems, he wasn't looking
forward to the press scrum as they fought to
get more information, or the next juicy titbit
about the couple.

Soraya groaned and threw herself back onto
the pillows. 'Could they not give us just one day
of rest? Last night was a lot.'

It was clear she shared his dismay about
the level of interest people would likely have
in them from now on. Aside from recovering
from the near fatal crash they'd experienced
last night, there were a few personal revelations they had to deal with too. The intensity
of the situation had forced their hand and made
them face up to the feelings they had for one
another and now they'd had one night together
he didn't think a fling was going to solve any
of their problems.

Far from ending a chapter in his life, last
night had opened a new one he was afraid he
wouldn't get to explore further.

It seemed their compatibility stretched beyond working together, and their emotional

bond, into the bedroom. What they'd experienced last night had been more than just sex. He'd had girlfriends in medical school, enjoyed the freedom of being a single man away from home. Then he'd met Zara and settled down into a long-term relationship. He knew the difference between a fling and something more serious because he felt it. The physical release of finally giving in to their desire for one another had satisfied him temporarily, but it had also awakened a stronger need to have Soraya in his life. She was beautiful, smart, compassionate, supportive, and sexy as hell. Everything he could ever want in a partner. Despite only knowing Soraya for a matter of days he felt a stronger connection to her than he'd ever had with Zara. And soon she would have to leave.

They needed time and privacy to discuss their relationship and that wasn't going to happen with the world watching and waiting to hear what was next.

It wasn't as easy as simply sweeping Soraya up into his arms and walking off into the sunset. Finding the woman of his dreams wasn't a guaranteed happy-ever-after and he didn't want to make the same mistake in giving his heart to someone who couldn't be there when he needed them. Soraya had her job in London, and her sister. He knew how the talk would end when the responsibility she felt for Isolde would never let her leave England for him. It wouldn't be fair to even ask her. Raed knew what he had to do. He just didn't have to like it. Nor did he have to do it right now.

'We might not have all day, but we do have this morning,' he said, voice husky as he reached for her.

Soraya gave a squeal of delight as he straddled her naked body, sending the tray of empty breakfast dishes tumbling to the floor. If he did have to let her go, he wanted to make more memories to keep him company at night.

'I'm glad you're finally back with us,' Raed joked with Duke at his hospital bedside.

'All thanks to you two, apparently,' he said with a weak smile.

'It was Soraya who did all the hard work. She was the one who probably saved your life.'

Soraya blushed at Raed's praise, even though she knew she deserved it. Although if she hadn't carried out the needle decompression to release the trapped air in Duke's pleural cavity, she was sure Raed was more than capable of doing it himself.

'How are you feeling now, Duke?' She diverted the attention back to the patient who, though his skin looked a better shade than it had last night, was still pale.

'Still in a bit of pain but I'm managing it with the medication they gave me.' He grimaced, but his discomfort was to be expected, not only because of the procedure, but also the after-effects of his crash injuries.

'Hopefully, after a couple of weeks' rest you'll be as good as new.' Thankfully there hadn't been any complications as a result of the needle decompression, so he should heal quite soon as long as he did as instructed by the medical staff on his release from hospital.

'That's what I've been told. Again, thank you. I also hear congratulations are in order for you two.'

Soraya glanced at Raed, who looked as uncomfortable as she felt as he mumbled, 'Thanks.'

'We should go and let you get some rest. Steve's on the mend too. They managed to save his foot but he's another one who needs to take it easy for a while. We just wanted to check in on you both to see how you were. You're both looking much better than the last time we saw you,' she joked, drawing a grin from Duke.

'That wouldn't have been hard. Apparently I was a very becoming shade of blue.'

'The same colour as Soraya's eyes.' Raed had meant it as a joke but it made her think back to this morning when they'd been lying in his bed staring into one another's eyes, without a care in the world.

An unexpected pebble of emotion seemed to lodge in her throat, bringing tears to her eyes. Soraya knew it was because that subject of where they were going next in their relationship still had to be addressed. They weren't hiding in bed any more and sooner or later they had to address the future. A conversation she knew was going to tear her apart when her loyalties, and heart, would be split between her sister and her lover.

'Anyway, we're glad you're okay and hope to see you on your feet again soon.' She practically stumbled out into the corridor with Raed in pursuit.

'Soraya? What's wrong?' He grabbed her gently by the shoulders and turned her to face him.

It was on the tip of her tongue to tell him she loved him, that she didn't want to go back to England without him. But that wouldn't have been fair on either of them when it hadn't been part of their agreement.

She was prevented from saying anything as they were suddenly accosted by a wave of men carrying phones and cameras rushing towards them.

Raed's face darkened with a frown. 'We need to get out of here,' he said to their new security detail.

Acting as a human shield, Raed once more put his body between hers and danger, bulldozing his way through the throng of press all shouting questions at them as they passed.

'When's the wedding?'

'Are you going to give up your medical career to become a princess, Ms Yarrow?'

'I—I haven't thought about that,' she stuttered. It wasn't something she'd considered, mostly because this was never supposed to have been a real relationship, and certainly not a permanent one.

'You don't have to answer them,' Raed warned, rushing her past as security fended off the few stray reporters in waiting further down the corridor.

'It's a question we should have prepared for. Our future.' It hurt to even think about it, a deep ache inside her chest at the thought of what might or might not come. No matter what happened between them, Soraya knew it was going to cause her pain. Even if they stood some chance of being together it meant giving up the life she had, her work and family, and risking it on another man. After Frank had left her so broken and devastated, she knew all too well the damage Raed could do if he didn't reciprocate the strength of her feelings for him.

Last night had been such an emotional roller coaster with the dinner, engagement, and the crash, but it had ended on a high. Being with Raed had been amazing and not just for the obvious physical reason. Though that would have been enough on its own for her to be distracted today. Raed understood her on a level no one else had ever come close to. Their backgrounds might be vastly different, but they had the same ethics when it came to work and family.

Frank had never grasped the importance of either to her. A spoiled only child, he'd had everything handed to him. One of the differences between him and Raed was that Raed couldn't wait to strike out on his own and support himself. Frank had simply substituted her for his parents to subsidise him. With everything Raed had done for his family, it was obvious he wasn't selfish like her ex-husband. He was willing to sacrifice everything he had in London to save them.

They'd agreed to continue with a short-term fling until Soraya had to leave the country, but she'd be lying if she said that would be enough for her. She was sure they could have something special together given time and wouldn't just walk away without attempting to salvage something of their budding relationship.

After Frank, Soraya hadn't considered the possibility of meeting anyone else, much less trusting her heart again when it had caused her so much pain in the past by loving someone so completely. Perhaps that was why she'd agreed to a short-term fling, in the mistaken belief that it would somehow protect her. The very nature of a fling suggested it was purely physical, no emotions involved. However, deep down she knew she'd been emotionally involved with Raed from the moment he'd broken down in her office.

Now she had to decide if she was going to make the break, or see if Raed was willing to try and make a go of things. One thing was for sure, a fling wasn't going to do her any good. It was showing her what they could have if he didn't have commitments elsewhere. Heartbreak just waiting to happen. She'd believed that a brief romance with Raed was better than nothing, but she knew it would only prolong her pain, make it all the more damaging when she had to say goodbye to him. Yet she couldn't find it in her to break things off now, before they were too involved, too smitten to think about the future and the repercussions of a separation.

Keeping her emotions to herself had been her way of protecting her family. She hadn't wanted her parents, or Isolde, to feel bad about the burden on her young shoulders. So she'd kept her worries and anxieties to herself so as not to worry them, something she'd carried on into adulthood, and her marriage. Even when money had been tight, Frank had been working later every night, and she'd kept her fears to herself so as not to rock the boat. As though her feelings hadn't mattered as long as he'd been happy. It wasn't until the end of their marriage she'd realised he'd never cared about her feelings when he'd run up debt and cheated on her. It had been a one-way relationship. If she wanted the pattern to change, to no longer be walked over as if she were a doormat, she had to make her feelings heard.

Raed's response to that would determine what happened next.

It wasn't until they were safely in the back of the car that Raed spoke again. 'I didn't think we had a future when you're going back to England tomorrow.'

Although he didn't want her to go, that one question from the journalist had jolted him out of his selfish reverie thinking their feelings for one another could solve all of their problems.

Soraya had a career and a family at home and
it wouldn't be fair to expect her to give them
up to be with him. He'd made that mistake with
Zara, expecting her to fall into place in his life
in Zaki, sacrificing everything in the hope they
could make things work.

He'd seen for himself last night just how
good Soraya was at her job, how she enjoyed it,
and how much she was needed in that medical
role. The reason he'd asked her to perform his
father's surgery in the first place was because
she was the best surgeon for the job. It would
be a waste of her skills, not to mention her future prospects, to give it up and trail around
the country behind him while he performed
his royal role. He didn't want to do it and it was
his legacy. She would only grow to resent him
the way he had his parents and his life in Zaki.

It wasn't that he didn't want to be with her,
quite the contrary, but it was too much to
ask of her to be with him. The sort of person
Soraya was, she would probably do it too and
he couldn't expect that kind of sacrifice on the
basis of one amazing night together.

'I was thinking about that. We're good together, Raed, it would be a shame to ignore that
fact. I know we agreed to a fling but maybe we
could extend things.' That smile and twinkle
of hope in her eyes made Raed's heart feel as

though it had bottomed out to join his stomach on the floor. In other circumstances he would be over the moon that she was willing to take a risk on him, especially after everything she'd been through with her ex. But it was a fantasy. He knew from experience it wasn't going to work. Despite his attempts to prove otherwise, his fate was to remain in his home country permanently. A life together just wasn't on the cards.

He didn't want to give her excuses, or reasons to think they could still salvage something. It would be better for her to make a clean break now rather than give her false hope that they had a future together.

If he tried to explain his reasoning to call things off, he knew she'd insist she could make her own decisions. The trouble was she wasn't so good at making the best ones for herself. It was time someone did right by her for a change now, even if it didn't seem like it.

'Listen, Soraya, I've been thinking about us...' His stomach plummeted with the task he'd set himself. 'I don't think it's going to work.'

'But—but...last night...'

Raed could see the pain in her eyes and hated himself for putting it there. He could only hope that if he ended things now she would forget about him quicker instead of his prolonging the hurt letting her think they ever stood a chance as a couple.

'It was great, but let's face it, Soraya, we'd just been through a lot. We found comfort in one another at a time when we were both emotionally fragile. It was an intense situation and we gave in to an attraction, but that's not the basis for any relationship, certainly not a long-distance one.'

They both knew their night together had been a lot more than that but admitting it left an opening for hope he couldn't afford. Soraya had spent her whole life putting other people's feelings before her own and now he was doing this for her. He'd tried so hard to avoid his legacy but embracing it now would help so many. At least he'd had a chance at putting himself first for a while, and now it was time to do something selfless. Even if it didn't feel like it in the interim.

'Maybe I could take some time off work and give us a chance to get to know each other a little better at least.'

The wavering in her voice and the glassy sheen in her eyes brought a lump to his throat and Raed had to cough to clear it before he spoke. 'What's the point, Soraya? I'm a prince with responsibilities to my country and my family. You knew this from the start and that's why we agreed to a fling. So things didn't get messy.'

The minute she'd been a listening ear and let him unburden himself of his worries that morning in his office, he'd known somewhere on a subconscious level that things were always going to get messy. Not least when he'd asked her to be his fake fiancée for the cameras. He'd known then he was attracted to her, there was a connection between them, and it was never just going to be a simple ruse. The pretence otherwise hadn't only been for the press. If he'd admitted to himself that there was something between them he would have tried harder to keep his distance and replace her with a stranger he would never have feelings for. But all of that was too late and now he had to pay the price.

'The point is we could have something special together if we only try. I'm not saying it's going to be easy—'

'And if I don't want to try? We scratched that itch, Soraya.' The bluntness of his words was a direct result of Soraya's attempts to salvage a relationship, but she would be the one expected to make all the sacrifices in the process and he wasn't prepared to let her do that.

He watched her swallow hard and blink back

the tears threatening to fall, despising himself for every second he was putting her through this. The only way he could get through it was to remind himself she would be better off without him, or his family's problems, holding her back. She deserved the quiet, anonymous life he'd been denied.

'Okay. I misunderstood the situation.' As the car finally came to a standstill outside the palace, Soraya opened the door and got out.

When she had to reach out her hand to steady herself on the door before she walked away, Raed's heart ached even more for her, but he remained stoic. Even when she turned back to face him.

'What about the engagement? The press? Has all this been for nothing?'

It was hard to look her in the eye but he did so in case she was in any doubt that this was over. 'We can just say things didn't work out and you're missing home. That should be enough of a story to cover my father's absence for a while longer. You can keep the ring. Use it as a down payment on your own house. You shouldn't be sleeping in anyone's spare room.'

'You have it all figured out, don't you?' she said with more than a hint of understandable bitterness.

'I appreciate everything you've done for me

and my family, Soraya. I never meant to hurt you.' His words fell flat as she walked away, unwilling to listen to his attempt at a too-late apology.

Raed waited until she disappeared inside, then he dropped his head into his hands, weary of all of the pretence. The pain in his chest was a just punishment for the hurt he'd caused one of the most amazing women he'd ever met in his life. Someone he knew he could never replace.

CHAPTER TWELVE

SORAYA WAS STILL reeling from Raed's abrupt dismissal two weeks later. She'd tried to put it out of her head and get on with the life she'd had before he'd crashed into her office that morning, but it was easier said than done. Even if she didn't still have press doorstepping her for an interview, thoughts of Raed and their night together haunted her. She yearned for the few days they'd had getting to know each other more than she'd ever done for her failed marriage.

'Will you stop mooning over that ring? Either sell it or put it away in a drawer where you can't see it.' Isolde snatched the emerald engagement ring from Soraya and shoved it in her pocket.

'It's not like I wear it. I just like to look at it sometimes and be reminded of Raed.' She pouted. It was all she had left of him now and sometimes it was better to recall the good memories than the pain and humiliation she'd felt when he'd ended things between them.

His actions had brought all her fears bubbling back to the surface that she was never going to be enough for the people in her life. From her parents' inadvertent neglect to Frank's cheating, no one had ever put her feelings first. She'd thought Raed was different, that he understood what she'd been through, that he would never hurt her. But he'd done just that in the most brutal fashion possible. Waiting until they'd spent the night together, until she'd trusted him with her heart and body and begun to believe they could have a future. In the end he'd been just like everyone else. Tossing her feelings aside for more important matters.

Okay, so protecting the royal family and running a country weren't trifling matters, but it hurt all the same. More so in this case because she'd been willing to take a chance on Raed after all she'd been through.

'I'll only give it back when you do as he suggested and put a deposit on a house with it. You can't live in my spare room for ever.'

'I'm sorry I ever told you about that…'

Isolde had made it clear that Soraya was suffocating her with her overprotective sister routine, and she suspected she'd outstayed her welcome at the flat. Isolde needed her space, and she was right, it was ridiculous that her big sister was still in residence, but she couldn't bring herself to sell the ring. Despite the circumstances around the engagement, she liked the idea he had been thinking about her when he'd chosen it. That there was some meaning behind the gesture other than a cover story.

'Raed did us both a favour by making sure you had enough gems to set up a new life. No offence, sis, but I enjoyed our time apart. I mean, I've loved having you live here but you can be a little…suffocating.'

Isolde wasn't telling her anything she didn't already know.

'I know, I'm sorry. I told myself I was moving in to save you. In truth, I think it was the other way around. I wanted to be needed.'

'I still need you, but not every minute of every day. I love you, and I appreciate everything you've done for me, but I can look after myself. It's about time you had a life of your own again.' Isolde gave her a soft smile and Soraya knew her words weren't intended to hurt her, even if they were hard to stomach right now. She'd thought she could have a life with Raed but he hadn't wanted her either.

'I suppose I can help out at the centre now it's up and running.'

Raed's cash injection for the charity had

likely been his way of salving his conscience, but it only made her think about how his kind-hearted actions were a stark contrast to the cold words he'd spat at her that last day in the car. Almost as though he'd been putting on a front for her, the way he'd done for the press, and his family. Being who anyone needed him to be in that moment.

'Raed wasn't all bad. Even if we're not allowed to talk about him these days…'

'You've changed your tune. If I remember correctly you wanted to chop off certain parts of him at the time and post them back to his home country one by one because he'd broken my heart.' The level of her sister's ire on her behalf had amused Soraya at a time when she'd been too devastated to think of such cold-hearted revenge herself. It appeared she wasn't the only protective one of the two sisters and it had given her a glow knowing she was loved by someone at least.

'Yes, well, the interview in the paper might have given me a different perspective on his behaviour.' Isolde lobbed the morning paper at her opened at a black and white grainy image of Soraya and Raed in the hospital that last fateful day in Zaki.

It was a special kind of pain seeing the image of him wrapped around her like her personal bodyguard, protecting her from the world. Soraya couldn't marry that selfless behaviour with his cruel parting words to her.

The headline—*Heartbroken Prince Puts Duty Before Love*—was accompanied by a posed picture of Raed, as handsome as ever but she thought he looked a little drawn. It was probably wishful thinking imagining he was pining for her the way she was for him.

"'When asked why his engagement had ended so quickly, Prince Raed would only say that his fiancée had a successful medical career in London and he had responsibilities at home. Although he wouldn't be pushed on the matter, it seems this distance proved a defining factor in the break-up, which has obviously left our beloved Crown Prince heartbroken..."' Soraya read aloud. The article went on to talk about his most recent public engagements, his new social initiatives, and praised him for his return home. She supposed playing the role of heartbroken beloved prince was gaining him some sympathy, and had taken the focus off his parents' absence after all.

Yet she couldn't quite believe it was all an act. It was the first time she'd heard mention of her career in the decision for their break-up...

Suddenly everything began to slot into place. He'd become distant right after that journalist had asked if she was going to give up her career for him.

'He got me to leave because he didn't want to make me choose between you and my job or him.'

'Of course he did.' Isolde rolled her eyes as though Soraya was the last person to understand his real motives.

Now she understood why he'd said those horrible things to her. He'd wanted her to despise him so she wouldn't stay in Zaki, knowing she'd be torn between wanting to be with him, and needing to stay for her sister. Not to mention her career. But it hadn't been his decision to make. If she hadn't been so consumed by self-pity, wallowing in the unfairness of sharing her life with the most selfish of people, she might have realised how out of character he'd been that day.

She'd simply believed he'd been following the pattern of everyone else in her life, had believed the worst of him and taken him at his word, when all along he'd committed to the most selfless act. Sacrificing everything, not only to save his family, but ultimately to protect her too. Without her even having to say the words he'd known she'd fallen for him and made the decision to walk away before things became serious between them. Raed hadn't realised it was too late, and her feelings for him had been cemented when he'd shown her that night just how much he cared for her.

'Why would he speak to the press about such personal issues when he works so hard to keep his feelings private?'

'Because he wants you to see it and realise he's missing you as much as you're missing him?' Isolde offered. 'You're very alike, you know, you and Raed.'

'How so?' Soraya had wanted to believe that, but when he'd gone back to take charge of his country she'd had to face the reality that they had nothing at all in common.

'You're both overprotective siblings who put other people's happiness over your own. It seems to me as though you look after family, and everyone else, because you never had anyone to do that for you. For once in your life someone was trying to do the right thing by you, even if he was being an idiot about it.' Isolde's smile said everything about her new understanding behind Raed's motives.

He'd gone the wrong way about everything, obviously, when it was Soraya he should have spoken to. Then she would have told him to stop trying to be so damn noble. That it was her happiness he was sacrificing along with his own.

'Then I guess it's down to me to tell him that.' For the first time in her life Soraya decided she was going to do something for herself and not worry about the consequences. It was time she concentrated on her own happiness, and she needed Raed to find it.

Raed's mouth was dry as he faced the bank of microphones and reporters gathered in the palace press room to greet him. He could've put out a statement through one of their public relations officers or done a one-to-one interview, but in the end he'd decided he should be responsible for answering the difficult questions so many people had about him and his family. With their consent he was going to put the record straight once and for all.

He took a sip of water and prepared to unburden his soul.

'Thank you all for coming today, and for your patience in waiting until I reacclimatised from the London weather.'

A polite titter emanated around the room. His return to Zaki had caused a stir, but he hadn't been able to face the public until now. A broken heart wasn't something easy to move past, even more so when he'd caused it himself. So he'd spent the past two weeks mooning around the palace like a lost soul haunting the corridors, not quite wailing over the loss of his love, but beating himself up over it nonetheless.

He'd thought time and distance, not to mention a whole new way of life, would have distracted him from his loss, but here on his own, save for the staff, he'd felt more alone than ever. The whole idea of getting Soraya to leave had been to lessen the pain of a long drawn-out goodbye later when things inevitably didn't work out. But by ending the relationship before it had even had a chance to flourish he was beginning to think he'd made a big mistake. The idea that his sacrifice would somehow make her life better, so she didn't have to adjust her life to fit around his, had spectacularly backfired, according to his brother. She wasn't happy with him, and Isolde apparently wanted to do unmentionable things to essential parts of his anatomy for hurting her sister. Understandable. He wasn't his own greatest fan at present either for making himself miserable in the process.

Raed cleared his throat. The sooner he did this, the sooner he could get back to the palace, which didn't give him the anonymity he missed, but was vast enough to hide away in.

'Several weeks ago my father, the King, suffered a massive heart attack while visiting family in London.' He ignored the collective gasp in the room and the flash of cameras, to continue. 'With subsequent surgery he is expected to make a full recovery. Until then, and with the consent of my entire family, I'm going to take over many of his public duties here. Are there any questions?'

The sea of hands in the air was expected but still overwhelming. He'd had the relevant media training for subjects he should avoid talking about, but he wanted to be as open and honest as he could be after all the deception and lies. It was exhausting just being here, never mind having to keep up the pretence. Especially when he didn't have Soraya's support, which had got him through some of the toughest days of his life.

'Yes, man at the front.' Raed picked out a familiar face who he knew had liaised with the palace in the past.

'Why was the news about the King's health kept from us?'

If Raed had hoped the journalists were going to go easy on him, the reality was beginning to set in. This reporter spoke for the whole country who wanted answers.

'We didn't want to panic the population. At that stage we didn't know if he was going to survive, and as a family it was more important to us to concentrate on his survival. As you know, both myself and my brother, Amir, have been living in England. With my father so ill we knew one of us would have to return, but neither of us wanted to leave the family at such a time, especially given the fact that we've already suffered great tragedy and loss. I'm sorry if our actions have offended or upset anyone. That wasn't our intention. We're human and it was concern for our father's well-being that was uppermost in our minds at the time.'

'Will you be returning to London once the King has recovered?' A slightly easier question from the woman in the knitted blue twinset he picked next.

'No. I'm staying here to take up my rightful place as next in line to the throne.' A ripple of murmurs in the crowd was accompanied by a stronger show of hands.

'Yes. The hand at the back of the room.' He couldn't quite see the journalist in question but the hand was bobbing up and down enthusiastically in the crowd.

'What about the rumours of your engagement?'

The question stirred more excitement in the room, including his. He wasn't sure if he was imagining the voice asking it.

'Unfortunately, that didn't work out.'

'Oh, really? Well, I have the ring to prove

otherwise.' The hand waggled the large emerald ring he'd so carefully chosen with Soraya
in mind, even though it was never supposed to
have been anything more than a prop.

'Soraya?' He stood up to try and see better. The crowd, bemused by the interaction,
began to part, leaving a straight path towards
the woman he'd convinced himself he'd never
see again.

'I left without saying goodbye.' She was
smiling as she walked towards him, so that
was a good thing.

'Well, long-distance relationships never work
anyway.'

'Not if you don't even try.'

'I was trying to protect you.' He slid his arms
around her waist, needing that physical connection to reassure him he hadn't conjured her up
out of his mind in the midst of his crisis.

'I didn't ask you to.' She grinned at him.

Raed wanted so desperately to kiss her, to
beg her for another chance, but he was aware
they were surrounded by the press and he had
something of his reputation left to hold onto.

'Then maybe we need to talk in private.'

The groan from the now invested assembled
press reverberated around the room, making
Raed laugh for the first time since Soraya had
left him. Perhaps he'd be forgiven for his past

mistakes if they got a new royal romance to focus on, but he wasn't going to take anything for granted this time.

'Thank you everyone for your questions and your understanding but I need to talk to my fiancée in private.'

He ushered Soraya to his private rooms, leaving his security team to disperse the reporters, hopeful that they had everything they needed for now.

'I hope that wasn't too presumptuous of me. To describe you as my fiancée, I mean.'

'It depends how things go, doesn't it? I don't even know if you want me to stay. I did turn up uninvited.'

'Of course I want you to stay. How did you get in anyway? Do I need to have a word with security?' He was only half joking. As much as he wanted Soraya here, he didn't want her safety jeopardised by lax security. Only pre-approved visitors should be admitted to the grounds, especially with a member of the royal family in residence.

'Your parents pulled a few strings for me. I told them I wanted to surprise you and I did save your father's life after all...'

'You've been talking about me?' He was surprised, but it also showed the bond she'd forged with his family that they felt comfortable enough, not only to discuss their relationship, but to give her security clearance without his knowledge. They must have been pretty confident he needed her with him to have agreed.

'Yeah, about how sad and lonely you are without me,' she said nonchalantly.

'They're not wrong.' Despite all the privileges and luxury available to him out here, none of it had made him happy. Only seeing Soraya again had done that.

'If it's any consolation, I was exactly the same.' She rested her forehead against his.

'I'm sorry. I thought it was for the best.'

'Again, something you should have consulted me on before coming to your own conclusion.'

'I thought by making that decision for you, it was saving you from having to decide between your life in England with Isolde, or one here with me. I know what it's like to be in that position and I didn't want to put you in it. I didn't want to be responsible for taking you away from your own family.'

'Again, my decision, and, as Isolde has reminded me, she's a grown-up. I don't have to put my life on hold to look after her any more.'

Raed raised an eyebrow at that, disbelieving that either of them would ever stop worrying about their siblings.

'I know, I know, but I'm trying. The thought

of losing you made me realise I want a life of my own too. Preferably one with you in it.'

Hearing that made his heart sing, though he was careful not to get too carried away again. 'But our circumstances haven't changed. My life is going to be here from now on, yours is in London. The logistics of a relationship are going to be tricky. Especially when I don't know what kind of schedule I'll have yet. In taking over Father's role in the interim I'll have public engagements and trips abroad to contend with. We might never get to see each other.'

'I'm taking indefinite leave from work. I'm dedicated to giving us a chance if you are. If we get sick of each other in a couple of weeks, I'll go home and back to work and put it down to an extended holiday. However, if we are as great together as I imagine, then I'm willing to move out here to be with you, Raed.'

She couldn't have stunned him more if she'd hit him over the head with a ten-pound mallet. It had never occurred to him that she would be willing to give everything up to be with him, because no one else in his life ever had.

'There's nothing that I would want more, Soraya, but it's a different lifestyle. I'm a prince, there are expectations, and the likelihood is I won't be able to return to my career as a surgeon. If we were serious, the same would apply to you. I couldn't ask you to give up your work for me.'

'You aren't, but you mean more to me than any job, Raed. I know the implications of getting involved with you—we've been there before, remember? But I'm willing to give us a shot if you are. If and when I move out here permanently, perhaps we can still do some consulting work or fund the next generation of surgeons. I'll do whatever it takes to make this work. Just give us a chance, Raed.' She was watching him with her big blue eyes, waiting for his answer. As though it had ever been in question.

If he'd ever been in doubt about his feelings for Soraya, the moment he'd seen her in that press room he'd known he was in love with her. Judging by the lengths she'd gone to, the risks she was willing to take for him, she felt the same. Finally someone loved him for everything he was, and he didn't want to let that slip through his fingers again.

'In that case, Soraya Yarrow, would you do me the honour of going on a real date with me? I figure we can't have a real engagement until we've had a real relationship.' And a real proposal. One that wouldn't be tainted by lies and pretence.

'I'd love to go on a date with you, Raed. I

love you. Or is that too pushy for a first date? I wouldn't want to put you off.' She was joking to cover the nerves she undoubtedly had over saying those words because he had them too.

'Not at all. I love you too, Soraya.' He kissed her, long and hard, trying to express just how much.

Her hands crept around his waist to hold him close as she kissed him back and Raed had never felt more like a prince in a fairy tale.

EPILOGUE

'WHO KNEW A life of luxury could be so exhausting?' Soraya laid her head on Raed's chest as they finally relaxed on the back seat of the limo.

He stifled a yawn. 'I did warn you.'

'Yes, you did.' From the time she'd first made her surprise appearance at his press conference he'd been asking her if she knew what she was getting herself into. The truth was that she hadn't realised how intense their life here would be, thrown into the spotlight because of his return as the Crown Prince, and their unconventional romance. However, his position had given them some fantastic opportunities to make a difference to the people here.

It had been only a couple of months since she'd decided to move over permanently to be with him and she didn't regret a moment of it. Yes, she missed her sister, but they spoke every night on the phone and she hoped Isolde would come over for a visit at some point. In Soraya's absence she was helping with the community centre project and relishing every moment of it. Soraya was so proud of her little sister, who had matured so much recently. Or maybe it had happened a long time ago and Soraya had been too busy trying to protect her from the world that she hadn't realised. Whatever the reason, they both seemed happier than ever.

'No regrets?' he asked, cuddling her closer.

'Definitely not.' In Raed's arms, his warmth enveloping her, there was nowhere else she'd rather be. 'I mean, living in a palace is a terrible hardship.'

His chest rose and fell as he laughed. 'We all had to make sacrifices. Seriously though, is this life going to be enough for you?'

He looked at her with such worried eyes that she knew the real question he was asking was if *he* could be enough for her. When all the while she was wondering the same about herself. She wasn't a princess, or from family of any note, but she loved him with all her heart. Whether he was living in a palace or a tiny flat, she knew without all doubt she wanted to be with him.

Raed was the most kind-hearted, loyal man she'd ever met and she considered herself a lucky woman that he'd ever asked her to be his fake fiancée. Even if the circumstances had been less than ideal at the time, it had given them the opportunity to spend time together getting to know one another and help each other move past the relationships that had caused them so much pain. Raed was everything she needed.

She sat up to face him so he could see for himself just how much she loved him and wanted to be with him. 'I know we've had to leave our medical careers behind in England for now, but we've already accomplished so much out here.'

His mother and father were back in the country now too, his father recovering well, but Raed was still undertaking the majority of royal duties for now. He'd become a popular figure with his new initiatives. Not only were they working on a centre for young carers here too, but he was also still in talks for a charity horse show to raise more tourism revenue. Even now they were just returning from a new food bank set up to help families struggling with the cost of living. Soraya was keen to set up a women's health centre too, where she hoped she could resume some medical duties when needed. They were still managing to help lots next year? I might have set a dangerous precedent here,' he joked.

But Skye's eyes glistened. 'I like a challenge,' she admitted. 'Maybe we have our wedding next New Year and the one after that…?' Her eyebrows rose as she laughed. 'Leave that one with me. I'll see what I can do.'

And Lucas picked her up and spun her around, kissing her the whole time. When he finally set her down, he grinned.

'All in your hands,' he teased. 'Surprise me.'

* * * * *

If you enjoyed this story, check out these other great reads from Scarlet Wilson

A Daddy for Her Twins
Nurse with a Billion Dollar Secret
Snowed In with the Surgeon
The Night They Never Forgot

All available now!